Early praise for *Tower*

An IndieBound Indie Next List Notable!

"Brutally poetic . . . Bruen and Coleman shine . . . displaying all the literary chops that have made their novels such cult favorites among mystery fans."
—*Publishers Weekly*

"Classic noir, add a touch of Richard Price and a dash of Higgins . . . With *Tower*, Reed Farrel Coleman and Ken Bruen slap you in the face. Noir, as well done as it can be is still not nearly as horrific as the evil that exists in this world. The proof is as it is written. *Tower* will singe and the pain is good."
—Ruth Jordan, *Crimespree Magazine*

"This book is a true gem! At times moving, at times witty, and always brilliantly decorated with the grit of the street, *Tower* proves beyond doubt that collaborative efforts can pay off like a million-dollar heist."
—Jeffery Deaver, best-selling author of *Roadside Crosses*

"Taking up the storied themes of crime fiction—loyalty and betrayal, temptation and treachery—*Tower* lifts and elevates them, forging a tale both barbaric and baleful, swaggering and broken-hearted. Brutal, soaring street poetry to take your breath away."
—Megan Abbott, Edgar Award-winning author of *Queenpin* and *Bury Me Deep*

"*Tower* would make an outstanding gift to anybody in the Witness Protection Program who is feeling nostalgic for the streets. Bruen and Coleman work great together—try to guess where one ends and the other begins. A rough and profane read, with haunting echoes of a Southie of the mind."
—Daniel Woodrell, Edgar Award-nominated author of *Winter's Bone*

"*Tower* is spare, powerful, surprisingly tender. And as seamless a piece of two-author writing as you'll ever find."
— SJ Rozan, Edgar-winning author of *The Shanghai Moon*

"Haunted by a genuinely unnerving sense of dread, this breathtaking, blood-dimmed tale unfolds with delirious, whiskey-soaked ferocity. Volatile and intoxicating, *Tower* blazes with a hardboiled intensity that is impossible to resist."
— Declan Hughes, Edgar Award-nominated author of *All the Dead Voices*

"With *Tower*, Bruen and Coleman deliver an unflinching, yet moving portrait of friendship in the face of blood, dishonor, and death."
— Peter Spiegelman, Shamus Award-winning author of *Red Cat*

"*Tower* is a fast getaway car of a novel—raw, brutal, and with enough Irish treachery to fill a hundred shamrock bars. If your taste is for hard-boiled, it doesn't get boiled any harder than by Ken Bruen and Reed Farrel Coleman in *Tower*."
— Thomas H. Cook, Edgar Award-winning author of *The Fate of Katherine Carr*

"*Tower* goes off like a slo-mo explosion, a raging blast of white-heat light. It's a compelling study of pathologies, and style, and friendship and fate. Fuelled by tenderness and murderous hate, it's as tender as it is brutal, tender as a savage wound, ragged and raw. Here be monsters, crippled monsters: Nicky and Todd are the truest angels and demons of our mean streets I've read for some time. Be afraid."
— Declan Burke, author of *The Big O*

"Great writing—the dirt of it, the hog of it—is less about telling stories than it is about recreating experience. When you read Ken Bruen and Reed Farrel Coleman, you're way out there past just reading stories, you're reading *lives*, lives that worm and burn their way into your own."
— James Sallis, award-winning author of *Salt River*

Also by Ken Bruen

Jack Taylor novels
The Guards (2001)
The Killing of the Tinkers (2002)
The Magdalen Martyrs (2003)
The Dramatist (2004)
Priest (2006)
Cross (2007)
Sanctuary (2008)

Brant novels
A White Arrest (1998)⁺
Taming the Alien (1999)⁺
The McDead (2000)⁺
Blitz (2002)
Vixen (2003)
Calibre (2006)
Ammunition (2007)
⁺—collected in *The White Trilogy*

Max & Angie Novels (writing with Jason Starr)
Bust (2006)
Slide (2007)
The Max (2008)

Other novels
Funeral (1991)*
Shades of Grace (1993)*
Martyrs (1994)*
Sherry and Other Stories (1994)*
All the Old Songs and Nothing to Lose (1994)*
The Time of Serena May / Upon the Third Cross (1994)*
Rilke on Black (1996) .

The Hackman Blues (1997)
Her Last Call to Louis Macneice (1998)
London Boulevard (2001)
Dispatching Baudelaire (2004)
American Skin (2006)
Once Were Cops (2008)
*—collected in *A Fifth of Bruen* (Busted Flush Press, 2006)

Edited by Ken Bruen
Dublin Noir (2006)

Also by Reed Farrel Coleman

Dylan Klein novels
Life Goes Sleeping (1991)
Little Easter (1993)
They Don't Play Stickball in Milwaukee (1997)

Moe Prager novels
Walking the Perfect Square (2001)
Redemption Street (2004)
The James Deans (2005)
Soul Patch (2007)
Empty Ever After (2008)

Writing as Tony Spinosa
Hose Monkey (2006)
The Fourth Victim (2008)

Edited by Reed Farrel Coleman
Hardboiled Brooklyn (2006)

TOWER

KEN BRUEN
&
REED FARREL COLEMAN

BUSTED FLUSH
♥♣♥♥♥ PRESS
HOUSTON 2009

Tower
Busted Flush Press, 2009

Author photo copyright © Ali Karim
Cover design: Jeff Wong

ISBN: 978-1-935415-07-7
First Busted Flush Press paperback printing, September 2009

BUSTED FLUSH
♥♣♥♥♥ PRESS
P.O. Box 540594
Houston, TX 77254-0594
www.bustedflushpress.com

Tower is dedicated to the memory of Anthony Fusaro.

ACKNOWLEDGMENTS

Ken Bruen
Thanks to Reed and David, brothers in so many ways.

Reed Farrel Coleman
Thanks to David for believing. To Phil Spitzer and David Hale Smith. To Al Guthrie. To Peter and Ellen. To Rosanne, Kaitlin, and Dylan. To Ken for giving me this chance.

PROLOGUE

"Always be near to them, but make sure they're far away from you."

—Jake Arnott, *The Long Firm*

GRIFFIN COUGHED BLOOD into my face when I made to slip the chains under his shoulders.

The chop on the water slapped the wrecked pilings with the backs of both hands and the thick layer of mist that hung over the West Side of Manhattan rendered the lights of Jersey a blur. They might well have been cleaning up the Hudson, but you couldn't tell by the stink coming off the river. Or maybe that was just the stink of Griffin's rotten soul.

"I forgive ya, boyo," he said through red, clenched teeth.

Stuck my fist against one of the two holes in his gut and pushed. Made his whole body twitch. Making Griffin twitch, now that was something to take pride in.

"Your forgiving me is pretty fucking funny. Like the devil threatening to send me to the principal's office. Besides, it wasn't me that killed you."

"I know that, but yer forgiven just the same."

"Sure he didn't shoot you in the head? You're talkin' kinda crazy."

"Do me a favor, Todd, don't finish me before ya put me back in the river."

"That's the one favor I'm inclined to grant. Why?"

"Penance. I've a long list of debts."

"You're a sick fuck, Griffin, and nuts if you think a few seconds of terror—"

"It's a start."

"For a guy had nothing to say while he was alive, you've become a talkative cocksucker as a corpse."

"Near corpse."

"I stand corrected."

"Look at me, boyo. Look close."

"What am I supposed to see?"

"Yer own self."

"All I see is a dead man."

"Then yer blind. Are ya sure yer looking close?"

I began threading the chains through the centers of my old weights. Pulled the chains tight and his whole body shuddered. Didn't like that, Griffin. Gave me the cold stare. The Griffin I knew.

"Fuck that, Griffin. I'm shitting my pants I'm so scared."

"Ya should be. Ya'll be here soon enough."

"Never."

"Look at me."

"Not this shit again. I'm nothing like you."

"The same."

"Nah, Griffin, I've never killed for pleasure, never detonated a car bomb and blown up toddlers and old ladies. Boyle liked telling people about that, scared the hell out of 'em."

"Yer missing the point."

"And you're pissing me off, Dead Man." Brought together two end links, slipped an old lock through, and clicked it shut. "Remember Jacob Marley, Griffin? 'These are the chains I forged in life . . .' "

"You'll be wearing 'em someday. They're God's commandments, boyo, not his suggestions. If ya think ya'll escape the chains, yer a fool. It's a tower of cards ya've built for yerself. Recognize the joker in the deck?"

Yanked hard on the chains to make sure they were secure. Griffin's body convulsed with such fury that he near rolled over. Few more episodes like that and he'd drop into the river without a push. The spasms calmed.

"Heard what you did to Rudi. Least I won't end up in a pile of lion shite."

"What, fish shit is more dignified?"

"S'pose we all turn up as worm shite one way or the other. Doesn't matter if a bullet finds ya or if a plane falls on yer head, you'll come out the ass end of something. That shield in yer pocket is no protection. Beneath the skin—" The convulsions began anew, struggle for breath. "Beneath the—"

Tapped my watch crystal. "Tick . . . Tick . . . Tick."

Said something to me, but it was barely a whisper. The blood bubbled and foamed on his lips. I put my ear close to his lips. Felt his faint breath. Kept my ear there. Waited. His breath grew fainter still. Turned to face him, my nose near touching his. His eyes were glassy, fixed.

"Nothing to say? That's the Griffin I knew in life."

His head jerked up, lips pressing against mine. Flailed to push him away, but his head fell dead to the pier before my hands touched him. Mouth painted red in his blood, I rolled him into the river, this time for a longer stay.

NICK

"HE BEATS ME."

One line, one simple sentence and I'm off.

Well, almost.

I'm sitting at the counter, peeling the label off a longneck, and the rage is filling my mouth, the bitterness rising like the old bile and I bite down, take a deep breath and try to ease a notch.

The deep breath helps?

Like fuck.

Debbie is the woman who works the bar, not bad looking, a bit of mileage on the odometer but who's counting? I can see the bruise under her left eye and it's going to blacken more in a day. I know, I've had my share and given them too. But not to women, never hit a woman in my goddamned life. Hurt them?

Yeah.

But that's a whole other trip and we'll get to that, like later.

I miss New York, every freaking moment and never more so than now. If this were Brooklyn or even downtown Manhattan, I'd be going to my car, opening the trunk, getting the bat out, taking care of business.

I guess I could say to her

"Suck it up."

It's what I've been doing for the past ten months and I'm sick of it. This one-horse shithole, this constant rain and the people, as miserable a bunch as you'd ever come across. So, the rain doesn't help their *disposition*, like I tell you now, that's a crock. You put this bunch down in Florida, you know what? They'd be bitching, it's what they do.

Whine City.

I say to Debbie

"Give me another brew?"

And she gives me the look.

Like, I'm not going to say anything about the shiner or what she just told me. Not today honey.

She sighs, plunks the bottle on the counter, and the way she does it, she's mad as hell. Disappointed too.

Fuck her.

Disappointment, honey, I wrote the book.

Ask my old man.

I look out the window, the grime-stained panes and I can see the arc of the mill. It's throwing a shadow, for all the world like the tower, the North Tower, where my old man worked.

That shadow has been with me all my life.

"What, you think I can't find a fucking supermarket? I've been living in Brooklyn seventy-five years. I know this city better than anybody."

—Jason Starr, Tough Luck

10 MONTHS EARLIER.

MY OLD MAN was as Irish as they come, Micksville in extremis. See that *in extremis*, so you know I'm not just some thug, I got me some learning. Not that I wanted it but my old man, he was a whore for books, always trotting out some shit, a book in his hand every goddamn minute. My Mom, she'd go

"Your father and books, don't get me started."

As if she needed an excuse. She was Jewish, she was born started. To say they were a poor match? Man, they were the worst marriage on the block and we had some beauties there. See the street on a Saturday night, after a ballgame and the brews had been sunk? Buckets of blood and recriminations.

Did the cops come?

Yeah, right.

Most of the participants were cops.

Mick neighborhood, what'd you expect?

I was christened Nick, after some Hemingway story. My old man loved him. His dream was to see a bullfight. I said to him one time

"What else do you think the hood is on a Sat night?"

And got a clip round my earhole.

He had big hands, the Irish inheritance, and though he was second generation, he was probably more Celtic than Notre Dame—the team, not the Cathedral. He'd been a cop for a while and he flat out loved it, then . . .

Got hurt in a drive by, pensioned out. That's when the bitterness set in.

Not that he was a bundle of good nature before. He was always a mean bastard, made him a good cop, but after the shooting, he peaked. Began to soak up the Jameson like a good 'un, and he'd have sat on his ass for the duration 'cept my mom, she rode him till he screamed

"Alright already."

The union got him a gig at the World Trade Center, a guard on the North Tower. The day, his first, a wet barren Monday, he donned the uniform, he went

"Bollix to this."

My mom, aiming for some peace if not calm, tried

"You look swell."

He was enraged, spat

"Fucking rent-a-cop."

One of the few times I ever agreed with him.

But he hung in there. A few years went by and he was promoted, still in the North Tower but pulling down more bucks.

And he liked it.

Not the job so much but he loved the building. Got himself a photo of his station, up on the 107th floor, and my mom framed it, put it beside Ariel Sharon and John F. Kennedy, over the fireplace. I said to my buddy, Todd

"The three stooges."

* * *

THE IRISH SURE have odd ways of looking at things, and the way they talk, full of twisted language. As if they see a perfectly good expression, then mangle it.

Why?

Fuck knows.

Maybe because they can.

Me, I figure it's all the Guinness, rots the brain and gives them that slanted view of the world. My mom, no slouch in the words department, would say

"Your father, like his race, they love the sound of their own voice."

Could be right.

What-the fuck-ever.

Like, who gives a rat's ass?

I can do a rap with the best of 'em but the difference, I try to measure the content. Not just shoot my goddamn mouth off. My teens, I started getting in shit, being rousted for nickel-and-dime stuff. My old man, he'd lose it, go

"You're a thundering disgrace. You're nothing but a punk."

The cops, cos he'd been on the job, would cut me some slack. Time came when that didn't work and I got sent to juvie hall. Hell with puke-green walls. I did six months and came out, hard.

The first thing my old man does, does he crack open a cold one, welcome me home?

He gets a hurly, sent from the heart of the old country, made from the ash, and gives me a flaking. I can still hear the swish of that wood as he swung it, the end walloping against my back and it hurt like a son of a bitch. He wanted to hear me cry. *Dream on you prick.* Finally, spent, sweat coasting down his face, he threw the hurly aside, said

"Let that be a lesson to you."

And he opened the Jameson, poured himself a serious one, knocked it back, said

"There's a chance I can get you on the tower, even with the sheet you've got. We can get it sealed but you're going to have to cut the crap."

I was picking myself up off the floor, pain everywhere and I looked him right in the eye, said

"Shove it."

Got another hiding. My mom, later, said

"Nick, he's got the bad drop."

She'd learned a few Irish-isms and she certainly got me nailed. I did what I do when I'm hurting, hooked up with Todd and we went to Park Slope, always lots of action there, had us some weed, and Todd had gotten tequila, boosted off a guy who'd hit a warehouse. We drank that, with Bud as back, and I went to that place, the cold zone, an icy territory I knew like the back of my hand, said

"Let's rock 'n' roll."

We caught a guy in an alley, fooling with some babe, and I used my feet, till Todd pulled me off, saying

"Jeez, Nick, enough. You'll kill the bastard."

I wanted to.

I can still hear the sound of the guy's teeth cracking, my boot hitting his mouth for the third time. Way I see it, you have to lay it off, get that poison out and maybe teach the guy something, like, stay the fuck out of alleys unless someone's got your back. Later, coming down, chilling, Todd passed me a smoke, lit me up, said

"You've got to rein it in, bro."

I asked him, not out of cussedness though there was some, but I really wanted to know, asked him

"Why?"

He sighed, shook his head, said

"You'll never last. They'll kill you or send you up for some serious time. You have to, like, ration it."

I dunno why, but that seemed to me hilarious. He stared at me, said

"You're one demented dude."

I moved out of Brooklyn shortly after, got a crash pad in the East Village and began my love affair with Manhattan.

Todd was into all sorts of scams: cards, hot goods, intimidation, muscle, and he got me taken on by a guy named Boyle, small-time racketeer. I began to pull in some change. Boyle was a big bastard and mean as hell. Took a shine to me, started to give me more and more work, usually boosting cars. I had a knack, could hotwire one in record time and be out of the street before you could count to ten.

Then the worst thing happened. Todd met a woman, went to South Philly with her. Didn't last too long, the woman that is. He came back for a week, then off to Boston, some business for Boyle. He ran with the gangs in South Boston, learned some moves with those guys and came back . . . quiet. I asked

"The fuck happened down there?"

He was drinking Jack D, Sam Adams as chaser, with a look of what I can only call controlled ferocity. He gulped the Jack, let it burn then

"Shit happened."

Fucking with those outfits, not the best idea.

He hadn't gotten a liking for violence, not like I had, but he definitely had a change in outlook, now he saw that sometimes you couldn't avoid it. One evening, on the Upper West Side, we were casing an apartment that Boyle figured was ripe for taking. We were doing the weed, nothing major, just mellow time and he started in on the Red Sox. He'd become a fan. Is there a bigger treachery? I shouted, the weed not mellowing me that much

"The freaking Sox? You're a Yankee's fan. The fuck you think you can switch like that? It's as bad as that asswipe who sold the Dodgers."

He gave a soft laugh, said

"Nicky, everything changes."

I came back with a reasoned, rational defense, a New York tolerance, said

"Fuck you."

We watched the apartment. The doorman went for a sneak brew on the hour and that would be our window. To get us back, to balance, I asked

"What's with that South gig, South Philly, South Boston, what's that all about?"

He didn't answer for five minutes, his eyes locked on the building, then

"Buddy, one way or another, the business we're in, everything goes south."

I blew him off.

He was right but by the time I knew that, it was all gone to hell in a shitcart.

I said to him, before we got out of the car,

"My mom, she says I've the bad drop."

He tasted that, let it hang. Like I said, he'd gotten this quiet gig going, then

"She's wrong."

I slapped his shoulder, said

"Thanks, buddy."

He glanced at where I'd touched him, a glance that warned

"Don't make a habit of it."

Then he said, real low

"More than a drop."

That evening went south.

*   *   *

I COULDN'T BELIEVE Todd picked the locks so easy at the apartment. I asked

"What the hell? No deadlock?"

Todd nearly smiled. Nearly. Smiling wasn't his strong point since Boston, said

"They got a doorman. Figure, why waste bucks on locks?"

I didn't get it, said

"I don't get it. They can afford the best."

We were in and Todd said

"Why? They're rich and us, why we rob 'em."

The place was a goddamn palace, could have put my whole neighborhood in the living room and the furniture, that white leather must be a bitch to keep clean.

Todd headed for the bedrooms, said

"Remember, cash, dope and jewelry."

I was staring at the art on the walls, said

"We're leaving this? This shit must be worth a bundle."

He snapped

"Pain in the ass is what it is. Can't fence it."

The paintings had little lights over them and I figured that must make them expensive. I was on the point of taking one when the door to the apartment opened.

*   *   *

TODD HAD PROMISED we were cool, no one would disturb us, the owner was a stockbroker, doing stock stuff. I heard

"The fuck is this?"

Turned to see a guy in a suit. If he was scared, he wasn't showing it. Todd came out of the bedroom, muttered,

"Fuck."

Shot the guy in the mouth . . . twice.

I was stunned. Of all the events I'd expected, this was not on the list. Todd was staring at his weapon, said

"Piece of shit, keeps jumping high."

I couldn't believe what I was seeing, went

"What?"

Todd indicated the gun, said

"I was going for a heart shot. Next time, I bring a Glock."

Next time?

The guy was lying in the doorway, his ruined head in the corridor. Todd walked over, grabbed one of his feet, said

"Gimme a fucking hand."

I did.

We stashed him in the bathroom, having dragged his ass across the carpets, blood trailing. The smell of cordite was heavy in the air and I went to the drinks cabinet, grabbed a bottle of Makers Mark, drank from the bottle. Todd protested

"Hey, not while we're working."

I pointed the bottle at him, asked

"What you gonna do, shoot me?"

He was hefting the gun in his hand, said

"If I have to."

I don't think he was kidding.

We put our haul in a black garbage bag and as we moved to the door, I asked

"Did you have to kill him?"

Todd, unruffled, glanced up and down the corridor, said

"Probably."

"Since the house is on fire, let us warm ourselves."

—*Italian proverb*

WE BROUGHT THE haul to Boyle. I was still reeling from the casual way Todd had offed the guy. Todd said
"There's a nice chunk of change in that."
He was driving with that total concentration, like he did most everything those days. I asked, sarcasm dripping,
"You got time to count it?"
He caught it, looked at me, asked
"What's with you?"
I wanted to lash out, grab him, shake some sense into him, tried
"You just killed a guy and you don't even mention it. We're going to act like it never happened?"
He reached into the glove compartment. For a mad moment, I thought he was reaching for his piece. Got his cigarettes out, fired one up, all fluid motion, his eyes never leaving the road, said
"It's over. What's to discuss? You want to dwell on it, replay it, do it on your own nickel."
I wanted a cigarette, a drink, some weed and mainly, the hell away from him. I cracked my knuckles, knew it annoyed the shit out of him, asked
"What happened to you in Boston, sorry, South Boston? I don't know you any more."
He shrugged, went
"Maybe you never did."
We were pulling up at Boyle's. Todd was sliding into a space right outside the warehouse that Boyle conducted business in, said
"Don't mention the shooting."
I laughed, not with any humor, asked

"You think Boyle's not going to hear about it?"

Todd was easing out of the seat, said

"No need to get into it now."

Boyle was known as Biblical Boyle but not to his face. We called him Mister Boyle. His tag came from his fondness for the Good Book. On his desk was a battered bible and he quoted from it, a lot. Pain in the ass is what it was. He was a comer, moving up from penny ante stuff to major league, had at least ten guys in his crew and had ambition. How he got to wherever the fuck he was going, he didn't care.

My life was crammed with Micks, my family and most of the guys I knew. Boyle was one of the most irritating. Third generation, he'd been to Ireland a few times and had more than once told me to get my arse over there, touch my roots. I assured him it was one of my goals but the only place I wanted to go was Miami. The warehouse had posters of Dublin and Galway, Galway with that Bay, and Boyle wasn't above singing a few bars of the song, "If I ever go across the sea to Ireland" and he sang like a strangled crow. In his late fifties, he had that barroom tan, the bloated face from too much Jameson, the busted veins along his cheeks. Small eyes that darted like eels and it would be a huge mistake to think the booze affected his attention. If anything, the drink seemed to work on him like speed for anyone else, got him cranked.

He always wore a crisp white shirt, tie and vest, the sleeves of his shirt rolled up, show he was a working stiff. He was running to fat but the arms were still formidable. He was sitting behind a massive desk, a wooden harp on the side and a family snap beside it, a team of kids and his wife, looking frightened. Probably with good reason.

Couple of guys were piling boxes and shooting the shit. Sitting in a hardchair, to Boyle's left, was his main guy, a genuine Mick, born in Belfast and rumored to have been with the Provos. Name of Griffin, he never said much, just stared at you with dead eyes. He'd never spoken to me but I had the feeling he didn't much care for me. I gave him lots of distance. Not that I was afraid of him, just, who needed the aggravation? Todd had cautioned

"Keep your eyes on Griffin."

And being contrary, I'd asked

"Why?"

Todd had sighed, as if he had to explain every damn thing, said

"Because he'll be watching you."

Boyle stood up, stretched out his arms as if he was going to hug us, and maybe if he'd had enough hooch, he might have. He said

"Me lads, back from their big adventure."

His accent grated on me. It was stage Irish. I was sure not even the Irish spoke like this. Todd put the garbage bag on the desk, the loot piled in. Boyle nodded to Griffin who moved slowly, took the bag, spilled the contents on the floor, began to sift through it. Boyle took a brief look, said

"Did good."

Then indicated two chairs in front of his desk, said

"Take the weight off, fellahs."

He sat down, reached in a drawer, took out a bottle of Jameson, said

"Wet your whistle?"

He placed three shot glasses on the desk, filled them. I reached over, took one. Todd didn't move. Boyle had his glass raised, looked at Todd, asked

"You're not drinking?"

Todd, in a lazy gesture, waved his hand, said

"Little early for me."

A look passed over Boyle's face, a tiny peek into what went on behind his eyes, and it was dark, malignant. He was still for a moment, then casually swept the glass off the desk. It narrowly missed Todd, the liquid spilling onto the cheap carpet. Todd never flinched, just sat there, his face without expression, as if dramatic gestures were so much smoke. Boyle said to me

"*Sláinte.*"

I knocked it back, waited for the burn. Boyle made a grimace, said

"Hits the spot."

Then to Todd

"Back home, you refuse to drink with a man, might be seen as an insult."

Todd gave a long look at the glass beside his boot, said

"We're a long way from Tipperary."

I thought Boyle might come over the desk but went with it, laughed, said

"Aye, you're right there, boyo."

Griffin was laying wedges of bills in piles and I saw a tiny smile. Fleeting but it was there.

Boyle stood up, said to Todd

"Get your arse down to the pier 80, I got some freight coming in."

Todd moved and I stood. Boyle said

"Not you laddie, I need you."

Then to Todd

"You can manage your own self. You have a mouth on yah for two men."

Todd had reached the door when Boyle shouted

"Any problem with that apartment?"

Todd gave it some thought, then

"Nothing major, Nick. Your laddie . . . had to shoot the owner."

Then he was gone.

Griffin was watching me, definite interest showing and Boyle turned to me, asked

"That right, you put a cap in some guy?"

My mind was reeling and I got out

"He walked in on us."

Boyle looked at Griffin, said

"Doncha hate when that happens?"

Griffin, as usual, said nothing. Boyle was putting on the jacket of his suit, an Armani, the real thing, you could tell by the way the jacket hung. He fixed the lapel, asked me

"You like the suit?"

I did.

On him it looked cheap. He was just a cheap guy, not all the clothes in the city were going to alter that. I said

"Class."

It was the right answer. I didn't look at Griffin. I knew he'd have the smirk in place. Boyle smacked me on the back and I don't mean a friendly pat, a hard wallop, said

"Stick with me boy, you'll have one yer own self."

I loved being called boy.

A gray Caddy was parked in the alley. Boyle threw me the keys, said

"Let's see what you got."

The fuck sat in the back, lit up a cigar, a Cuban he said, and it smelled cheap. Not unlike the cologne that he smothered himself in. He gave me an address in the East Village, said

"Swing by the Towers, we'll see how your old man's doing."

My heartbeat accelerated and Boyle laughed, said

"Just fucking with you kid. Had you going."

He did.

I liked being called kid as much as I liked boy. As we swung into the Village, Boyle asked

"How's your old man? He doing okay as a rent-a-cop?"

Now that's exactly how I saw my father but I didn't much appreciate Boyle calling him so. He laughed again, said

"Look at the face on yah kid. You could explode. I like a bit of spirit. Now your buddy Todd there, he's a cold cunt."

The obscenity as icy as the sentiment. I put the car in park, got out and waited on the sidewalk. Boyle didn't move, then the window rolled down and he asked

"The door gonna open by itself?"

He wanted me to open the door?

He did.

Biting down, I grabbed the handle, eased it out and he lumbered towards me, said

"You have a bit to learn yet."

The smell of the cigar was overpowering and if that came from Cuba, we'd been sold a crock for longer than we knew.

We went into a brownstone and I headed for the stairs. Boyle laughed, said

"Whoa there Butch, we're going down."

Butch?

My first surprise was to see Griffin already there. How the hell had he managed that?

The second was the man tied to a chair.

He looked familiar and then it hit me, the doorguy, the man who'd been on the front in the Upper East Side, who'd fucked off for a drink. His face was swollen and he looked at me with pleading in his eyes and I was thinking a line of shit

How'd he end up here?

What the fuck was going on?

And pleading, the fuck did he think I could do?

Boyle smiled, said

"Nicky, meet Mr. Slovak, recently custodian of the prestigious address you knocked over."

Was I supposed to shake hands, ask

"How you doing?"

How he was doing was pretty bad.

Boyle gave him a casual slap on the back of the head, almost friendly. Griffin was watching me with those dead eyes and I noticed pliers in his left hand, and fuck, blood on it or was it rust? Jesus, I thought, be rust. I knew, call it instinct, that a guy like Griffin, his tools would be pristine.

Like that word, "pristine", got a ring to it, right?

Yeah, them *Reader's Digest*s, worth their weight in . . . whatever.

Boyle went to a small cabinet, took out a bottle of Jameson, two glasses, poured stiff amounts, handed one to me and said

"We're gonna drink to this bollix, this fuckhead, who was supposed to call up if the owner returned. Mr. Slovak got the bucks in advance, cos I'm like an upfront kind of guy."

Griffin gave a snort like a bull in heat, not a sound you'd want to hear a lot. I avoided meeting his eyes and Mr. Slovak, well, he sat on, going nowhere, no appointments to meet and he may have whimpered but I think that was my imagination. I fucking hope so. Boyle continued

"Our lookout, our representative if you will, what's he doing, he's knocking back the old vodka or whatever shite they have in his homeland. I'll bet he's sorry he came to the land of opportunity now. So he's soaking up the sauce and the owner returns, leaving me boyos unprotected."

He looked at Slovak with, I swear, something like concern, like, you doing okay there buddy? Then clinked his glass with mine, said

"*Sláinte amach.*"

The Irish toast. I'd heard my old man use it like a zillion times. I muttered

"Back at yah."

Not meaning a word of it and tossed back the hooch. It took a second then it burned, oh yeah, just the way you love it, like a sweet lady rubbing your belly, the belly of the beast . . . jeez, I'd had three . . . four? . . . serious drinks in the last hour and was beginning to feel them. I'd be needing them.

"No snapshots of life flashing before my eyes, thank fuck. I mean, thank God. Devout, that's me."

—Ray Banks, *The Big Blind*

I'M SKIPPING THE whole deal with the doorman. You wanna know why? Cos I can . . . well, I can blot it out. Gimme enough Makers Mark or, better, some of that Tennessee hooch, Knob Creek, I can blot out almost anything, even Shannon.

Shannon and her little boy. He was ten years old last Wednesday. Happy birthday little buddy. I taught him how to play ball and for a Down Syndrome kid, he could throw pretty damn good. I think of him, I get an ache above my left lung, from the bullet hole, I tell myself.

It was three days after Griffin went medieval on the doorman's ass. I was in Rocky Sullivan's, the joint on Lexington? Yeah, Irish, I know, but what you gonna do? Todd asked me along, he had a hot date . . . well, hottish. Babe from Long Island, I forget her name and I guess Todd forgets it too. Rocky's specializes in writers and music. Lots of bands from the Old Sod wash up there and writers, they say you ain't arrived till you read there. I'd heard Eoin Colfer read there once. Guy had a nice deadpan humor.

That evening, it was open mike . . . Yeah, you know that lame gig, comedians, poets, singers, whoever, get up there and strut their pathetic efforts. It sure gets you drinking and I didn't need a whole lot of excuse. The scene in the basement was Technicolor in my mind. Jesus, the blood when Boyle took off the poor bastard's first finger . . .

I was sinking Jim Beam, Sam Adams back. Todd was chatting to the babe, extolling the freaking Red Sox. Real smart, bring out a woman and talk sports? He glanced at me as I ordered up a fresh batch, muttered

23

"Whoa, slow down there tiger."

I want to think the babe smiled but she was one of those, she figured it would spoil her lip gloss. Yeah, you get the picture. Cute, huh?

I raised my glass, said

"Here's to the Yankees."

Followed it with a chug from my bottle of Sam Adams. He didn't respond, looked at the narrow stage as a tall girl strode up.

A moment.

One split second, your whole life changes. What went before is barren and you're grabbed by a feeling you never knew existed. I don't believe in love at first sight. Lust maybe, sure, why the fuck not, but love? Yeah, right. But that's what happened. The woman, in her late 20s, with long auburn hair, wearing blue jeans, boots and a tank top, wasn't pretty in any conventional way. Her face had lots of flaws, trace of acne, too long a nose, but hell, cheekbones to die for and she turned for a second, as if assessing the crowd and I saw her eyes, the strangest color, green with flecks of gray and a slight narrowing of her focus, as if she was short sighted. You'll have gathered I'm a hard ass, not a guy to fall for schmaltz or airy fairy shit but she hit my heart like a goddamn wallop. I actually gulped and like how often is that going to happen?

Smitten.

Good word that. I like it and that's what I was, right from the get go. Signed, sealed and delivered, baby. Fucked, in other words, and total. Here's the odd thing. Todd caught it, or spotted something, looked at the woman, then back to me, said

"Who'd have believed it?"

I didn't answer him, didn't want that moment spoiled. She took the mike, said

"This is a Neil Young song."

And launched into

"Powderfinger."

I swear by all that's holy that I'd heard that song, lots of times. Who hasn't?

No biggie.

Now, now it was alchemy, and okay, bear with me here, it sounds like jerk-off rapping but she glowed in the rendition and I could feel Todd's eyes on me, I wouldn't look at him.

Would you?

Then she did a Tom Waits song and she was done. Rapturous applause. They fucking flat out loved her. I pitied the bastard who had to go on next. How could you follow that? She went to the bar, started talking to another woman, took a hefty belt from a long neck, no glass, my kind of woman. And I was up, moving towards her, asked

"Can I buy you a beer?"

Without turning, she said

"Fuck off."

* * *

DID I PUSH it, grab her, ask her

"Where's your goddamn manners?"

Nope.

I slunk back to my seat, tail between my legs, whipped and Todd asked

"Strike out, huh? Just like the Yankees."

I gave him my granite look, feeling cold fury rising and drained my Beam, shouted at the waitress for another round.

Todd's lady nearly smiled and my evening had gone right down the shitter. Did I take it well?

Like fuck.

Proceeded to get loaded and get myself geared to kick ass, any ass. Todd stood, said

"We're outa here. Share a cab?"

I glared at him and he warned

"You don't want to stay here, why don't you just call it quits? We can hit a club."

I waved him off and he shrugged, said

"You take it easy buddy. You don't wanna do something stupid."

Oh, yes I did.

But first I had to pee. I had to edge past the bar. She was still with her friend, a guy on stage mutilating the English Language with some tribute to Ginsberg. She asked

"What's the matter with you, you give up that easily?"

Her voice was soft, a slight rough edge but she'd put work in, hard to tell she was from the Bronx. I stared at her, said

"Babe, life's too short for you fucking with my head."

She laughed, a rich full one, said

"The amount of booze you're sinking, your head is already fucked. And don't call me babe."

I pushed on. Who needed this crap? The restroom was packed, guys pissing away the week's wages. A guy shoved against me, knocking me, threatened

"Watch your step, fellah."

I hit him fast and low, said

"Sorry."

Then unzipped, let all the beer shower over the dude. His buddy, washing his hands, asked

"The fuck you doing?"

I glared at him and he let it slide. I was kinda sorry.

I came back, feeling vented in every sense, and as I passed her, she handed me a cold one, said

"*Sláinte.*"

I took the bottle, asked

"You're Irish?"

She raised her eyebrows, went

"Duh, *hello*. It's like a Mick bar. What were you expecting, Romania?"

Fucking mouth on her, she had to be a Mick, just what I needed. I put the bottle on the counter, said

"Shove it."

And went back to my table, downed some more Beam, simmered afresh. I don't remember much after that. Those blackouts, a curse and a blessing. Most times, the former.

I woke in my own bed which is miraculous enough, and better, alone. Times, I woke, saw my bed partner, wondered what the hell I'd been doing.

Yeah, that rough.

I was in my clothes so no surprise there and a greenish leg of chicken testified to late night munchies. My stomach heaved and I hit the bathroom, tore my jeans off, checked the pockets and found a slip of paper. Written on it was

Shannon

You need to lighten up

And a phone number in the city.

I muttered

"The fuck is that chick at?"

Todd had told me no one calls babes chicks no more, but then he also switched from the Yankees, so like, how much notice was I going to pay him?

Six Advil, a gallon of water, two strong coffees and I was good to roll. Good-ish. Todd and I were to hook up in the Village for another job for Boyle. More and more, we were spending our time on his business. It was starting to pay serious bucks and I was able to give my mother some cash. My old man, seeing me do it, barked

"You've got a job?"

I didn't answer. No reply was going to satisfy him. But he wasn't through, said

"The boys tell me you're jobbing for that Boyle."

The 'that Boyle' was loaded with contempt. The boys were his buddies from the force. Course, I should have known they'd be on it. I looked at him, asked

"So?"

He wasn't able to take his hand to me no more, I was too big, but his face let the thought show. He spat

"Piece of shit hoodlum, gives our race a bad name."

I decided to fuck with him, said

"He's been to Ireland three times this past year. How many times you been, Dad, like, in your whole life?"

None.

And well he knew it.

Always meaning to, if. . . fucking if . . . the lottery came through or he stopped drinking or the Knicks could win another goddamn championship. My mother intervened

"Will ye stop it? I've a nice stew made, and for once, could we just have some peace to enjoy it."

Yeah, and pigs might fly or the Brits pull out of Northern Ireland.

The stew was thrown against the wall shortly after and I stormed out, Sunday as usual. Happy families on a Brooklyn afternoon.

Todd was leaning against a Buick, a Pall Mall in his mouth, said

"You're late."

He had a half smirk building and I figured he'd gotten laid with the lip gloss queen. I asked

"Score?"

He flicked the cigarette high, watched it spin then flutter to the sidewalk, opened the door of the ride, said

"You sure as hell didn't."

He was pulling out into traffic and I went

"Shannon, that's her name."

Surprised him and he gave me a brief appraisal, said

"You're shitting me."

"Nope, I got her phone number too."

He cranked the radio. An old Heart song came on. I sang along in my head. High school, I always had a thing for them. He nodded, said

"I know her."

I let that sit then

"Yeah?"

"Yeah, used to run with an old buddy of mine. She's got a kid, a damaged one, something wrong with him. Like mental stuff."

I didn't know what to do with this information so I did nothing with it. We were parking alongside a deli and he said

"She's a ball buster. Way too much broad for you."

He indicated I was to get out and I volleyed

"Broad? No one calls babes broads any more."

I think he gave a slight smile, least that's the way I want to remember it. I asked

"What's the deal?"

He straightened his back. He'd hurt it in Philly and it gave him lotsa grief, said

"Guy owes some vig."

I wasn't packing anything save attitude, asked

"He gonna be a problem?"

Todd pushed the door, said
"Let's find out."
He was.

* * *

I LOOK BACK on those days and I'm not proud of what we were doing, but hey, we had to eat. The deli guy, big mother with beefy arms, sneered at Todd, said

"Two-bit punk, you come in here, expect me to hand over my hard-earned dough. The fuck is the matter with you? Can't you find some decent line of work?"

Todd looked bored, even a touch apologetic, which was him at his most unpredictable. He fired up a smoke, blew a perfect ring, said

"You got kids in school, over at St. Mary's, right?"

The guys face went nuclear. He roared

"You threatening my family, you no good piece of shit? Get the fuck outa my place before I come over the counter."

Todd dropped the cigarette, didn't stub it out, said

"Hey, no need, I'm coming over myself."

And vaulted the counter in one fluid movement, his back not troubling him then and had the guy in a neck choke, a cleaver under his lips, said

"Want me to take your tongue out?"

This brought back the scene with the doorman and I felt bile rise in my throat. The only two customers were edging towards the exit. The deli guy had balls, I'll give him that. He managed to spit, the phlegm landing near my shoe. Todd said

"I love it, a hard case."

And he dug the knife into the guy's neck. Let it sit for a moment then let him slide to the floor. He grabbed an apple, took a huge bite, said

"Tangy."

And we were out of there, back in the car, burning rubber. I was trying to catch my breath, and finally managed

"Gee, that was smart, killing him."

Todd let the window down, flipped the apple core out and said

"It looked worse than it was. An old Boston trick. They think you severed the jugular but it's only an artery. No biggie. He'll have a re-focus and presto, the payment will come through. You get your neck slit, it narrows your agenda."

I didn't know who he was anymore, if I ever really had. We'd been buddies so long, I never gave any thought as to whether I actually liked him. At that moment, I fucking flat out hated him. He lit another cig, asked

"So, you and Boyle. Tight, huh?"

I savored that, much as he had the apple and sour. Oh yeah. I said

"He doesn't much like you."

Todd laughed. Went

"Who the fuck does?"

But he was right. The following week, the deli guy came through.

*   *   *

I CALLED SHANNON, my palms covered in sweat, a chick making me nervous. She answered on the third ring and I said

"It's me."

A slight intake of breath, then

"I'm going to need a little more than that, fellah."

She knew, course she did. But hoops, I had to jump through 'em. I sighed, then

"Rocky Sullivan's, I liked your singing, tried to buy you a brew."

Another beat, then

"Oh, the drunk Mick. What do you want?"

Jesus.

I nearly slammed the receiver down and how different everything would have been. I wouldn't have spent ten months in this forsaken shit hole for one but . . . what? . . . I was determined to get the better of her, said

"Hey, you're the one put your number in my pocket."

She laughed, that rich sound, said

"I guess I was a little shitfaced me own self, you think?"

And the whole tone of her voice changed. I arranged to take her to a movie the following night. She said she'd meet me on Fifth and 33rd. It crossed my mind that I could have collected her but maybe she didn't want me to see the damaged kid. I asked myself

"So, her having a kid, how's that sitting with you all?"

Not easily.

* * *

DRESS TO IMPRESS.

Good base plan but the little voice in my head cautioned that she wasn't going to be easily won over. If I wore a suit, she'd spit on me, that was a given. Too casual, she'd think I didn't give a flying fuck.

And I did.

So I went to The Gap. You might look like the all-American asshole but at least a tidy one. Chinos, Converse All-Stars, not too new, scuffed along the sides, like I'd been shooting baskets, and a navy blue shirt, accessorize my eyes. A hooker told me that and for a hundred, I felt like believing her. She didn't of course let me kiss her on the mouth, they never do. Give you a blow job but kissing on the lips? *Fuggedditaboutit.*

I debated my Yankees jacket but didn't really want to get into a whole biggie about sports, settled for my battered bomber leather. It had loads of pockets so that was a plus, gave me an Indiana Jones vibe. Tiny hint of cologne, gotta ration that shit real slow or a chick will have your ass, you smell better than her. Checked myself in the mirror, all the young dudes, and gave my hair a careless flick, get that outa bed gig. Hummed Wham's "Careless Whisper" and I was out of there.

She was late. Gee, what a surprise and when she finally showed, I said

"You're late."

She stared at me, then

"What happened to 'Hello, you look nice?' "

She did, look nice, real nice. White jeans, black T-shirt and Keds. A light tan set the whole deal off. I was standing outside the movie, pointed at the times, said

"We've missed the opening."

She clutched her heart, said

"Oh no, how can I go on?"

Then she linked my arm, said

"C'mon. I'll buy you a beer and you can do guy stuff like talk about yourself for three hours."

I smiled in spite of myself.

It was one of those golden New York evenings, not too humid, a light breeze off the Hudson and a buzz in the air. She said

"Let's walk till we see a place that sings to us."

Is there an answer to this, an answer that seems related to logic?

She wrinkled her nose, said

"Whoa, buddy.   Got a little carried away with the aftershave."

Fuck on a bike.

She squeezed my arm, said

"Just jerking your chain. You smell real nice."

And found ourselves on West 44th, the Mansfield Hotel, across the road were The Algonquin and The Iroquois. She said

"James Dean slept there."

Like I gave a fuck where he slept. Her face had taken on a wistful look. She added

"You look a little like ol' Jimmy, you know that?"

I said

"Jerking my chain again."

She stopped, looked me full in the face, said

"Hey, someone gives you a compliment, you go, thank you very much. Okay, you down with that?"

Like I was going to get into a big thing about some fucking dead movie star. I let it slide with

"Whatever."

She ran a hand through her hair, something I wanted to do and badly, said

"You're a defensive guy, anyone ever told you that?"

I was tired of losing every round so snapped

"Maybe I've got good reason."

Like that was going to fly.

She was right on it.

"And what, the rest of us don't? *Hello?* But guess what? We're out for an evening, want to have nice time, we bend a little. You think you can do that, bend a bit?"

The hell with it, I said

"Like a blade in the wind."

We settled on The Algonquin, and the first thing I saw was a fat white cat on a pillow, in the lobby. I don't mean a guy in a suit, I mean your actual feline. We went into the bar, got ourselves a window table and before we ordered, Shannon asked

"You read?"

"Sure, the *Daily News.*"

"What happened to the bending?"

I had a Bud and she went for a glass of white wine, saying

"It's that kind of place."

I was thinking it was just another tourist trap and checked the bar list, said

"Sure do know how to up the ante."

She gave a tiny smile, said

"Class is always going to cost."

Which is a crock and did I say so?

Nope.

She was toying with the wine. I'd sunk the beer and fast, ordered another and she covered the rim of her glass. What? I was going to force her? Not sure if it was the smart thing, I asked

"So your kid, how old is he?"

Her eyes lit up, no fooling. I thought that only happened when you snorted some particularly fine coke. It was like she was shot through with energy and you know what? Goddamn it to hell, I felt jealous, of some dumb-ass kid I didn't even know. I wanted her to light up like that for me.

Dumb, huh?

Her words came out in a torrent, spilling over each other in their joy.

"Sean, Sean is eight now. He's a real tough little dude. He's got Down Syndrome. When he was born and the doctor told me, I thought my world was done. My heart was crushed, a handicapped kid, and me . . . *me* . . . to look after him?"

The brightness in her eyes was shadowed. A touch of, I dunno, self-recrimination. She continued

"You know about mosaicism?"

Yeah, right.

She nodded, explained

"It's a type of Down's that means he's not affected mentally but physically," and God forgive me, she actually made the sign of the cross. Jeez, I hadn't seen that in a while, then

"If I had to make a choice, I'd have him mentally all right. The physical side we can work on and we do."

I decided to go for broke, get it out of the way, asked

"His father?"

She reached for the wine, drained half, gulped, then

"Jeff's not the worst."

The Irish, they say that, like I'd heard my old man do, they mean you're a shithead. I figured I was doing okay, batting an even five hundred fifty, pushed

"And Jeff, you see him?"

She gave me a look like, was I serious? Said

"He's Sean's father, course I see him."

Fuck.

Then she focused and spat

"Oh, I get it. You're asking do I, like, sleep with him?"

Well, yeah.

I protested, a bit too much but she waved it off, said
"None of your fucking business."
So I figured, yeah, she was balling him. I wanted another
beer but she said
"You know, I'm going to call it a night. Got to get up
early for work."
I'd fucked up, yeah, screwed the whole deal. Outside, she
hailed a cab, asked
"Drop you?"
Wasn't she already doing that?
I said
"No, I'm good."
She reached over, kissed me full on the mouth, said
"I'd ask you to come home with me but you probably
don't on a first date. So call me, we'll have Friday night, a
real whoopee evening."
And she was gone.
What did I think? Fuck knows, nothing positive.

* * *

BOYLE BROKE MY nose.
Wallop.
Right across the desk, out of nowhere.
One minute, I was sipping an espresso and next, I was
jumping up, hot coffee burning my crotch and the pain of the
damned in the center of my face. He was asking about the
deli owner and I'd said
"No prob."
Griffin of course, was standing to his right and I was
keeping my eye on him. Boyle was resting his hand on the
good book, had earlier quoted me a piece from Revelation.
It was a revelation to me that the fuck could read.

Then he'd lunged across the desk.

He sat back, massaging his knuckles, adjusting his tweed vest, said

"Do I have your attention?"

Griffin was smiling. Looked more like a rictus. I tried to get my eyes in gear, the pain in my burned crotch as bad as the sledgehammer to my nose. A trickle of blood poured into my mouth. I mumbled

"Yes, sir".

Thinking, you fucking bastard.

He tossed some tissues at me, said

"Now clean up and get your head straight."

I went to the restroom, and in the mirror, saw my nose slanted to the left. It was already swelling. I managed to stem the blood but wouldn't you know, I'd elected that day to wear a white shirt. Not white no more. Electric stabs of agony were shooting to my startled brain. I cleaned up as best I could and returned to the office, trying to rein in my rage. Boyle was laughing out loud, something Griffin had told him. He shook his head, as if to rid himself of frivolity, said

"The guy who ran the deli, he could have gone to the cops and the last thing I need is heat. You get what I'm saying?"

I nodded and even that drew pain from my face. He gave me a long intense look, then

"That's going to give you a bit of character. Make you seem like a tough guy. You want that, eh, be a hard arse?"

How on earth do you answer that, especially to the man who just re-arranged your features? I mumbled something about wanting to do the best I could by him, brown-nosing, if you'll forgive the play on words, telling myself, suck it up, your time will come and we'll see about toughness. My old man had his nose broken in a street brawl and I don't know if it toughened him but it sure soured him. At last we had something in common.

I nearly missed Boyle's question.

"Your buddy, Todd, how tight are you guys?"

Figured out that this was loaded so went for

"He's a Red Sox fan, what can I tell you?"

And Boyle loved that, slapped the desk, the fuck, always slapping something, said

"Fucking turncoat, the likes of him, back home . . ." He meant Ireland. Home was freaking Hoboken ". . .we call them informers. They dropped a dime on us every time we got a rebellion going, sons of bitches. How you going to trust a cunt who deserts the Yankees?"

Griffin was quivering. This was obviously where he lived. Anything to do with betrayal, hatred, got his mojo cranked. Boyle indicated him, said

"You're going to be trailing along with my Mr. G this evening. How'd that sit with you?"

Not good.

I was hoping to have another round of verbal warfare with Shannon. I said

"That's cool."

Griffin spoke, his voice startling me

"Be here at 7:00 sharp. Wear black."

Despite my nose or because of it, I shot back

"A funeral, is it?"

Levelled those ferret dead eyes on me, said

"Will be if you fuck up."

"You didn't know that each time you passed the threshold you were saying goodbye."

—Colson Whitehead, *The Colossus of New York*

GRIFFIN WAS DRIVING a beat-up Chevy. He was wearing a black suit and looked like an undertaker. How apt that was? There was something dead about the guy, not just the eyes but his whole face had the sheen of the embalmed. He was wearing some kind of god-awful cologne. One of those scents that a guy gets hold of early in life and is convinced is a winner, despite all the evidence. Made you want to gag. But with him, perhaps that was the point. I had a cup of coffee and he said

"Sling it."

I had been about to take a sip and I paused, asked

"Do what?"

He put the car into gear, slid out into traffic like a hearse, slow but deadly, said, without looking at me

"You deaf? Lose the cup."

We were in midtown, heavy gridlock and I went

"You're kidding."

Griffin, whatever else, a kidder he wasn't. He gave that grimace smile, as if he'd swallowed something vile, said

"No one, no fucking one, smokes, drinks or eats in my ride."

I rolled down the window, the full container in my hand and slung it.

I couldn't resist, asked

"Happy now?"

He liked that, I could see by the slight tensing of his body. He said

"I don't do happy."

Gee, what a surprise.

When I didn't reply, he said

"We're going to swing by the boss's old lady."

And dumb-ass I was, I asked

"Mrs. Boyle?"

He cut in front of a yellow cab, nearly rear-ending the guy, scoffed

"Jaysus, you know nothing, do you?"

I was tempted to say

"Well, I know you're a total prick."

But figured it would keep. He said

"Mr. Boyle's bit of stuff. She's been stepping out and you know, the one thing you don't want ever to do, is screw around with him."

So I asked

"And we're going to what, throw a fright into her?"

We were on the triangle below Canal Street. Tribeca, bounded on the other side by Murray Street, transformed into a vibrant mix of commercial, lofts, studios, galleries and chic restaurants. He pulled into a disabled parking spot, said

"Get out."

I looked at the street sign, Franklin, and what I knew about it was it cost. You had a place here, it was serious bucks. We stood before a renovated building, and Griffin took out a set of keys, let us in. Course, I had to ask

"You have a key to her place?"

He ignored the elevator, took the stairs, said

"I have keys to everything."

Second floor, a brightly painted door, had little flowers on the top. He sniggered, then knocked. There was the sound of music, Whitney Houston? Then a woman's voice,

"Who is it?"

Without missing a beat, he said

"Fed Ex."

There was a peephole and she could obviously see him. She opened the door. The first thing she did was sigh and I was with her there. Griffin at your door, you'd sigh too. She was barely twenty, barefoot, in halter top and jeans, her hair wet, like she'd just been in the shower, and she was a looker.

Oh yeah.

Puerto Rican maybe, that brown sheen, glistening, and that was almost funny as Boyle was, like so many Micks, a raging bigot, spitting invective about niggers and tar babies, sand Arabs and spics. If she was intimidated by Griffin, she was hiding it well. Put her hands on her hips, demanded

"'Cho want, Griffin?"

Before he could respond, she let her eyes settle on me, asked

"Who's the kid and who moved his nose?"

Griffin was enjoying it, especially as he knew what was coming down the pike. He didn't even look at me, said

"The hired help."

She dismissed me thus. Riled me? Yeah, a little. Griffin had a scan around the apartment, all leather furniture, covered in plastic for the most part and I tried not to see Boyle, Bible in one hand, mounting her on the couch, probably wearing his socks. Micks and their socks, like Texans and boots. Griffin made a big production of shooting his cuff, checking his watch, a Tag Hauer, and he wore cuff links. I mean who, apart from freaking Donald Trump, wore them any more? You could see they were tiny harps, the whole Irish variation of wearing your heart on your sleeve. He went

"You've got, lemme see, okay, one hour to get your arse out of here, pack up your shite and get the fuck gone."

She was stunned, took her all of a minute to digest it then, eyes blazing, she retaliated

"You cho don't tell me to move. Only Papi does that, he want me to move, he come here, be a *hombre*, tell me hisself."

She'd balanced herself on the balls of her feet, ready to ignite. I stood well back, hoping to fuck she'd launch, tear the smug bastard's eyes out. Griffin was delighted with the reaction, put his hand in his jacket, said

"Chickee, you've been screwing around. You think you can give it away when the boss is paying for exclusivity? I have a little going away pressie for ye, so you don't, you know, go away, empty handed."

He took a vial from his pocket. You could see a liquid rolling in there. He unscrewed the top and before anyone could act, he threw the contents in her face, said

"Acid, baby. Like your tongue."

It wasn't.

Just ordinary tap water. But for one horrendous moment, she and I were believers. My response was

"Holy fuck."

And she, she clawed at her face, shrieking

"*Dios mio, madre del Jesus.*"

Religious reaction all around, you might say.

She sank to her knees, sobbing, all the spunk gone out of her. Griffin hovered over her, tapped his crotch, said

"You're down there, you want to give me one for the road?"

If I'd been packing—and why the hell wasn't I?—I'd have shot the bastard. I did find my voice, said

"Enough."

He turned to me, smiled like a cobra, then back to her, said

"I was wrong. I said an hour, the clock is ticking, *mi puta*, so you got, what, forty five minutes? The next time, it won't be water."

And he walked out of the apartment. I went to her, asked

"Are you okay?"

Christ, was I kidding?

She managed to look up, her face a ruin of fright and rage, spat

"What kind of *hombre* are you?"

Good question.

* * *

I GOT IN the car. Griffin said

"You give her a little comfort, you do that, fellah?"

I was too agitated to answer. He put the car in gear and we burned rubber. We pulled into Boyle's. Griffin took out a set of keys, asked

"How'd you like to live in Tribeca? Nice place, huh? You can see yourself there?"

I was taken aback, asked

"You're giving me her place?"

He shrugged.

"You want it or not?"

I couldn't get a handle on this, tried

"So who'd I have to kill for that?"

Without missing a beat, he said

"Your buddy, Todd. Kill him, the apartment is yours."

He had to be even more deranged than he seemed. I gasped, then

"Why on earth would I kill my best friend?"

Griffin was opening a packet of cashew nuts, tore at the cellophane, put a pile in his mouth, chewed loudly and I wondered what happened to the no eats in the car rule. He said

"Because he's a cop."

How did I respond?

Badly.

Very.

I followed Griffin into Boyle's office, my mind a pit of savagery. I wanted to kill someone, Boyle and Griffin topping the poll. Boyle was chewing on a hot dog, grease dribbling from the corners of his mouth. He'd a large bottle of Dr Pepper, and gargled from that, all of it in stereo. Between bites, he asked

"So, how did it go, kid?"

I looked at Griffin, and Boyle said

"Don't be scared kid. Speak up. I don't much like scaredy cats."

Where the fuck did he find that? Was it possible he'd heard of Dr. Seuss?

Naw.

I cleared my throat, always a sure sign you're about to pop a whopper. I said

"Mr. Griffin got the job done."

Can you believe it?

Like the girl asked

"What kind of man was I?"

Boyle spluttered his drink and even Griffin seemed amused. He said

"I like it. You got *cojones*, kid, you know that?"

The good book as usual was resting on the desk and wiping his leaking mouth with his sleeve, he opened it, read

"Then when lust hath conceived, it bringeth forth sin; and sin, when it is finished, bringeth forth death."

He looked up, his face shining, a mix of grease, sauerkraut and fervor. Mad bastard. He asked

"You got a copy of this here volume?"

Oh sure.

I was going to say

"Caught the movie."

But went with

"Yes, sir."

I have no reason, no explanation for my next action. I shot my cuff and *looked at my watch.*

Fuck.

Few insults to equal it.

Instead of taking offense, Boyle squinted, asked

"What's that you're wearing?"

Was he blind? I nearly said

"Like, hello, it's a watch, one of those items, got little hands, like you. And you know what, tells you the time, how cool is that?"

I said

"A Timex, sir."

Bought it off a guy in Times Square, cost me all of ten bucks but what the hell, it did the job. Boyle sat back as if he'd never heard such a thing and I was thinking, hey fellah, it's far from any freaking watch you were reared, sounding eerily like my old man, not a good thing. Boyle got a toothpick, dug deep into his teeth, extracted some meat, popped it back in his mouth, said

"Be-Jaysus, no one in my crew is going to be a cheapskate. Lemme see."

Pulled open a drawer, rummaged round then took out a watch, offered it across the desk.

My jaw dropped. I thought that was an expression, like in books and shit, but I could feel my face droop.

A gold Rolex.

Griffin was amused at my reaction. Boyle said

"Don't just gape at it, try it on."

I did.

It fit, like sin.

I shook my wrist the way you do and the thing slid nicely along my wrist. Was it my imagination or did it sparkle?

Boyle said

"'Tis yours, I look after my lads."

I didn't know what to say. Part of me was thinking

"Is it one of those knockoffs?"

Boyle said

"'Tis the real McCoy, none of that cheap imitation with me."

I said

"I dunno what to say."

Griffin said

"Thank you would be nice."

The fuck.

I muttered

"Mr. Boyle, I'm very grateful."

He was taking the wrapper of a cigar, lit it with a Zippo, blew a cloud of smoke at me, asked

"How grateful?"

What?

His tone had completely altered, his mood swings as mercurial as Irish weather. A nasty edge had leaked all over his words. I wanted to ask

"How grateful am I supposed to be?"

Boyle scribbled something on a sheet of paper, handed it over, said

"This is my tailor. Get yer arse down there, get some decent suits. He'll be expecting you."

I did some more lame gratitude and he waved it off, asked

"You gonna grease this cop for us?"

I wanted to sling the Rolex at him, said

"He's my buddy."

Boyle grimaced, looked at Griffin, then

"Cops ain't nobody's buddies. He doesn't know we're on to him. We're gonna let him run a bit then I want you to put a cap in his head. You do that for me?"

Stalling, I said

"I'll do it for the Yankees."

He loved it.

He tossed a set of keys across the desk, said

"Welcome to Tribeca."

"Straight to Hell."
—The Clash

THOSE DAYS, I was big into The Clash, had all the imports, direct from London. "Rock The Kasbah" was on my headphones day and night. Took Shannon out and she spotted the Rolex, asked
"That real?"
"Naw, a knockoff."
She didn't believe me but let it slide. I was wearing one of the new suits and she asked
"What is it you do?"
"Import export."
She digested this, then
"A gangsta, huh?"
Pronounced it with the full hip hop flavor.
I shrugged it off, said
"Yeah, that's me, a real hood."
Her face took on a serious bent and she said
"I don't want to be messed up with some penny ante hoodlum."
I wanted to point at the watch, ask
"That penny ante to you?"
We'd been out for a meal, and it went well. Our barbed, spiky banter had eased a notch and we were getting if not comfortable, at least a little more familiar, but as long as the sexual tension hung over us, there was a vibe. As if reading my mind, she said
"I'm going to sleep with you."
What do you say?
"Fucking A?"
I said in a serious tone
"I'd like that."

And she stared into my eyes, went

"Like? You're going to love it."

O-kay.

So, I asked

"When?"

And here was the kicker.

"When you get to know my boy a little."

The following Sunday, I took them to the park, had me old baseball mitt and got the kid playing. He was a quiet little guy but he sure could hit. Took him a time to get the swing of it but he soon began to smack the ball back and I said

"Right out of the ballpark."

He had a way of looking at you that hit at your very heart and I liked him, liked him a lot, told Shannon and she said

"I know."

We were getting there.

Two days later, I got shot.

* * *

I ARRANGED TO meet Todd in a tavern in Brooklyn, not Manhattan. If I was going to confront him then it was going to be where we grew up, let the betrayal seem more stark.

Fucking cop?

Jesus wept.

I now had a piece, courtesy of Griffin. A Browning .45 automatic. He'd said

"Try not to shoot yer balls off."

At the last minute, I didn't bring it. I'd moved into my pad in Tribeca, and felt, I dunno, like a fraud. Didn't belong there and the other tenants, meeting me briefly, seemed to agree. One prick, I said

"How you doing?"

He gave me the look, the one I've received all my life, that goes

"Shouldn't you be coming in the service entrance?"

Yeah, like that.

Tempted to give the Browning a trial run with him and he asked, in a snotty tone

"Are you delivering something?"

I counted to ten and beyond, said

"I live here."

He moved back, no kidding, stepped back a pace, said

"We'll see about that."

Enough.

I grabbed him by his shirt collar, asked

"You threatening me?"

He pushed my hands away, not a touch intimidated, said

"That's not a threat, that's a promise. I'm on the building board. We have certain standards. I wasn't informed we were allowing garbage men to sublet."

Can you believe it?

I gave a short laugh, said

"Oh, I'll be taking out the trash buddy and you'll be it."

He swaggered off, with the parting shot

"Don't unpack."

Jeez, can you believe that shit? I felt like a kid again, at school, when the nuns walloped the holy fuck outa me, just for the practice and I wanted to scream

"What'd I do?"

Song of my life . . . . *what'd I do?*

Bollocks to them.

For my meet with Todd—Todd the informer, the goddamn snitch, the turncoat—I put on the Armani suit. Yeah, I'd been to Boyle's tailor.

Wore a silk shirt, black slip-on cordovans, a tie with the Yankees Crest, splashed on some Tommy Hilfigger cologne, slid the Rolex on my wrist, liked the give of it, and checked myself in the mirror. Said

"Look like a player, buddy."

Nearly believed it. Last item, I guess I better get it fessed up, I was doing a little nose candy, nothing major, not then, not like I had me a jones or anything but hey, gave me that icy dribble down the back of my throat, and apart from the first blast of a cold one on a humid New York evening, few feelings like that.

Hit my brain like the A train, hard and cold, lightning up my mind. Took a moment, listened to Strummer with "London Calling," then got the hell outa there.

I was behind the wheel of the Buick. Yeah, Boyle's. And remembered, sitting on the sink, the Browning, locked and loaded and forgotten.

Shit, blame the coke.

I do.

Met Todd at Moe's Tavern, a neighborhood joint, run by a guy named Micky Prada, a straight shooter if ever there was one. Micky took one look at me, did a double take, asked

"That you Nicky? The fuck you doing, working on Wall Street?"

Couple of the regulars, they got a real kick outa that. Freaking losers, still hanging at Moe's. I dunno if there ever was a Moe. Micky had always had the bar. I flipped him off, asked

"You got Seven and Seven?"

He laughed.

"Seagram's and Seven up? Jameson no good for you no more?"

"Gimme the goddamn drink, alright?"

He poured out a measure, a slight tremor in his hand, and I was glad to see that, slammed it on the bar and I said

"Run a tab. Todd's coming by."

One of the jokers at the counter, said

"Yankees choked, you hear?"

I gave him the look, asked

"You hear me talking to you? I ask you anything?"

He rolled his eyes and I grabbed the drink, moved to the back to watch the door. The snow was cruising in my skull and when the booze hit, I felt the jolt. Reason I did the gig. I was cranked.

I was on the other side of my second drink, thinking of maybe another line of powder when Todd showed. He strode in, wearing a battered leather jacket. Pressed jeans, who the fuck ironed jeans?

He did some high fives with Micky. People always liked Todd. Well, except for Boyle and Griffin. He had that effortless charm, when he wanted, an easy grace that said

"You're the person I most want to talk with."

A crock, but hey, it worked.

He grabbed a cold one, came over, surveyed me, said

"The yuppie in all his glory."

We were off.

I spat back

"Wouldn't hurt you to make an effort the odd time."

He took a hit of the beer, belched, said

"What you thinking, if I suck up to Boyle, he'll dress me too?"

The tension was in the air, a slice of barbed wire you could almost touch. He watched me for a moment then

"What are you on? Doing lines in the men's room? Getting a taste for the finer things, that it?"

I indicated my glass, said

"A shot of decent booze. That's a big deal?"

He leaned back, his scuffed boots making that sound of intent, said

"The pupils of your eyes, they're pinpoints. Only one thing does that."

Time to rumble and I leaned close, said

"That one of the things they teach you in the Academy, one of those cop instincts you've developed?"

It hung there, like dead smoke.

But he was cool, I'll give him that, shrugged, said

"So you know about that."

As if I'd accused him of pinching a couple of bucks, like, no biggie. He was the ice man. I wanted to reach over, smack him up the side of the head, and if I'd been carrying the piece, I swear I'd have taken it out, pistol whipped him. And okay, the coke and 7s weren't helping my *disposition* but I was so fucking enraged. My old man, Irish to the bloody core, he had an expression all the way from Galway, to describe serious anger: *spitting iron.* Well, I was ready to vomit pure steel. Todd reached up his hand, signalled to Micky, said

"Yo, another round buddy."

I gritted

"I'm not freaking drinking with you, you . . . cheese-eating rat motherfucker."

And he smiled, a small crease between his eyes. I knew that signal. He had it when he was amused but on the verge of aggression, as if it was sad but kind of funny too, like life just wouldn't quit being a bastard.

The whole expression asking, in a Brooklyn accent

"Watchagonnado?"

He grabbed my arm, real bad move and said

"Listen up you hothead, you listening?"

I was.

He said

"Boyle is a major bad ass. He's into heavy shit and we've been monitoring him for a long time. The guy in the Upper West Side, the guy I wasted, he was one of ours and the guy in the deli, again, one of ours. It was a set up. You really think I killed that guy or that I'd cut a man's throat? But we had to make you believe. You buy it, then Boyle would buy it. This a big operation, Boyle is even running with the IRA. And also doing deals with some very nasty dope dealers, South of the Rio Grande."

He took a thirsty slug of his beer. I'd never heard him give such a long speech and then he continued

"Boyle's told you I'm a cop, so even though it's fucked that he's rumbled me, it's good that he's bought you as one of his crew. What's he want you to do, waste me?"

And gave me that level stare.

My mind was awhirl. He *was* a cop. I'd been suckered every which way but loose and he was sitting there, full of himself. I said

"Fuck you. He reamed me a whole new asshole, yeah?"

He put the beer down, said

"Whoa buddy, I'm watching out for you. Your back is covered all the way."

Micky brought the drinks and what the hell, I sunk the Seagram's neat, felt it burn like acid, then I asked

"All the goddamned lies, the Red Sox, that part of it too?"

He nearly smiled, went

"Hell no, that's the truth. They're going to take the series within the next few years, see if they don't."

I felt tired. The coke was winding down. Needed another line, shit, a whole battalion of 'em. I asked

"You do me a favor?"

"Name it buddy, it's a done deal."

"Get the fuck out of my sight. Now."

He sat back, like in recoil but slow, then stood, laid a mess of bucks on the table, said

"I'm here for you buddy but if you're thinking of running with Boyle and offing me, think again."

Then he was gone.

Moe's had one of those big ole Wurlitzer jukeboxes, and one of the regulars fed it a pile of quarters and Lou Reed began with "Walk on the Wild Side." I stood up, added a couple of bills to the tab and started to walk out. Micky shouted

"Don't be a stranger, hear?"

The evening had gotten cold or maybe it was the cocaine chills. I began to button my jacket and the bullet took me high in my chest, knocked me back against the tavern, and as I slid to the sidewalk, I could still hear Lou crooning about all the colored girls

Catchy little tune.

"He says, 'Times are changing. Men are afraid of women. I know a lot of beautiful women who should be with men, but you know what they're doing now?'

'What?' me and Roz want to know.

'Whacking off alone in their beds with vibrators . . . I have seen the future and it hums . . .'"

—Julia Phillips, *You'll Never Eat Lunch in This Town Again*

I OPENED MY eyes, a dryness in my mouth and an ache in my head, my chest. Turned my head. Bad idea. The nausea struck and realized I was in the hospital, Todd sitting shotgun by my bed. I croaked

"Come to finish the job?"

He was slumped in the chair, a long black duster gathered round him, his scuffed cowboy boots stretched along the floor. He sat up, his eyes tired, went

"You think I shot you?"

"Did you?"

He reached for a jug of water, poured a glass, offered it to me, said

"It was me, you wouldn't be here giving me grief."

He tilted my head, got some water in my parched mouth. I tried to gulp it and he pulled back, said

"Whoa, easy. You don't want to take too much. You gotta ease down slow."

A drip was attached to my right arm and my head really burned. He said

"You were thrown back against the wall. Knocked your fool self cold."

The door burst open and I mean burst, not opened gently. My mother, hysteria in full riot, going

"My baby, are you all right?"

Then whirled on Todd.

"Where were you, you shit? Where were you when they were pumping my baby full of holes?"

Jesus.

I tried to get my voice level, said

"Mom, I'm okay, really, you don't need to fret."

Whoops.

She was off.

"Not fret? And what about your poor father, he's near had a heart attack, what about that?"

I wanted to go

"Oh, like sorry, I'm goddamn shot and he's what, upset?"

I said

"Will he be coming by?"

Like an echo, she went

"Coming by? The poor man couldn't eat breakfast."

God forbid he miss a freaking meal.

She looked at her watch, a cheap plastic job my old man gave her for their anniversary. I checked my wrist, no Rolex, she went

"I've got to get back to your father. . . ."

And was gone.

I wanted to shout

"Where's my grapes, my bowl of restoring stew?"

The door opened, a guy in his fifties came in, wearing a battered sports jacket and his whole weariness screamed *the heat*. He nodded at Todd, produced a badge, gold one, asked me,

"You up to a few questions, Mr. Barrett? I'm Lieutenant Ortiz, OCCB."

Todd stood, said

"I gotta scoot. I'll drop by later."

A look passed between him and Ortiz. A cop look?

And Todd added

"With grapes."

Ortiz pulled up a chair, asked

"Mind if I sit?"

And if I did?

He took out a notepad, said

"Your old man was on the job?"

I nodded and rang the call button. The pain in my chest was fierce. A nurse appeared, asked

"How are we today?"

Who, me and Ortiz?

I said

"I'm hurting, like, real bad."

She tutted, like she didn't believe a word of it, said

"The doctor will be doing his rounds shortly. I'm sure he'll prescribe something."

And she began fluffing the pillows. They learn that in nursing school. When in doubt, fluff the freaking pillows. I snapped

"They're fine."

She gave me that tolerant smile you give precocious kids, said

"Bit cranky are we?"

And was gone. Just like my mother.

Ortiz gave some form of laugh, more a snigger then said

"You're one of Boyle's crew?"

I stared at him then said

"So?"

He flipped a page of his pad. How many pages did he have on me?

Then

"You lie down with scumbags, you're gonna get flak."

I tried to act like this was priceless information and made *mmm* noises. Mainly as I know how fucking irritating it is. He fixed his eyes on me, the cop special, asked

"Any idea who'd want to take you out?"

I shrugged and he added

"Next time you might not be so lucky."

He stood up, then

"Lemme give you a bit of advice, sonny."

I drank some water, noisily, and he said

"Because of your old man, we're cutting you some slack but don't depend on it. You're a punk and when we find your sorry ass in an alley, you think we're gonna shed any tears?"

He headed for the door and I said

"Forgot anything?"

Got to him and he frowned. I said

"Where's the bit about not leaving town?"

He put his pad in his jacket, wiped at his mouth and said

"You have a mouth on you, you know that? But if I had a nickel for every two-bit shithead with an attitude, I'd be rich."

* * *

I'D HAVE FUCKING killed for a double espresso and a line of coke. Or a clean shot of Bourbon. Jesus wept, I was in pain. The doctor swept in with a retinue of cowered nurses, interns or what the fuck ever those trainee doctors are. I said to myself

"Incoming."

I'd been on a diet of Nam movies: *Apocalypse Now, Go Tell the Spartans* . . . not *Platoon* though, that was like Nam lite. I had me an obsession with Coppola. Knew the dude did forty cups of espresso a day. How fucked is that? Made me like him even more, cos I dug it. He fitted in with my whole world view: fucked.

The doctor checked my chart, without turning to the horde huddled behind him, said

"Gunshot wound, above the heart."

I cut through the shit, asked

"What happened to 'Good morning and how are we today?' What happened to that gig?"

One of the followers gave a suppressed laugh and the doctor whirled, shouted

"That funny, you think a gunshot is funny?"

Jeez, talk about a heavy number. He moved toward me, examined the wound, made *mmm* sounds which told me absolutely nothing other than that I was in deep shit. He stood back, said

"You can leave today. The dressing will need to be changed daily. Come back for a check up in five days."

Then he turned and walked out, the posse scuttling behind. I wanted to shout

"God bless."

After the nurse changed the dressing, and I attempted the breakfast, I asked for my clothes.

She indicated a wardrobe, said

"Your shirt had to be thrown out but your jeans and jacket are there. Your friend, the one who got you this *private* room, he left you a clean T-shirt."

Her tone hinted that she was not fond of people who got special treatment. I opened the closet and in all its red glory, was the T with, you guessed it, *The Red Sox.* I turned it inside out, preferred to look stupid than Boston, which might amount to the same thing. I was pulling my boots on, groaning, when Shannon walked in. She looked tired, circles under her eyes and her hair like she couldn't find a brush. I'd have finger combed it for her. She appraised me, said

"You look shot."

I stood up and felt a slight wave of dizziness but that might have been down to her. I asked

"How'd you know I was here?"

"It was on the news."

I didn't know, was she angry, sympathetic, what? Her words had an edge but then, they usually did. I asked

"Want to walk me off the premises?"

I signed the release forms and she stood at my side, then

"Why are you wearing your T-shirt inside out?"

Before I could answer, she moved her arms round me and kissed me full on the mouth, to the delight of a passing nurse. Pulling back, Shannon whispered

"I'm so sorry."

I blew it off, went

"Hey, it's just a flesh wound, no biggie."

She was shaking her head, said

"No, I mean, it's my fault."

I moved a step, looked at her, tears in her eyes, and asked

"You shot me?"

She took my hand, said

"Let's get a cab, get the hell out of here. I hate hospitals."

We got the cab and a surly driver. Shannon gave her address and then slumped back in the seat, said

"Jeff, my ex. He shot you."

Real conversation stopper, that.

* * *

HER APARTMENT WAS in North Brooklyn, the Polish enclave of Greenpoint. This had in recent years become the über-trendy merging of North Williamsburg and Hasidic South Williamsburg. The building was in good shape, lots of flower boxes on windows, bright painted doors, an air of bohemia but with cash. I asked

"You afford this?"

She shrugged, said

"My dad owns it."

I hoped he lived elsewhere, like, maybe Ireland. She added

"He's a carpenter, and real smart."

He owned this building, I believed her.

I went to pay the fare. The driver pointed at the meter. I said

"Bit steep."

He hawked some phlegm out the window and if I'd been more focused, I'd have made him eat it. I paid and he looked the tip. I asked

"What's the matter, not enough?"

He growled

"Guess it'll do."

And before I could slap the fuck, he burned rubber outa there.

Cabbies, you gotta love 'em.

Shannon's apartment was on the ground floor, clean, full of light and the evidence of her little boy all around. Pac Man, Sesame Street Posters, small sneakers thrown on a couch, *miniature* baseball bat, and heart rending, a crayon sketch of a stick figure on the wall, with, underneath *my mom.*

I said

"Looks just like you."

She couldn't keep the joy from her eyes then, nervous, asked

"Get you something?"

"Jeff's address?"

And lowered the tone, brought the boom down on whatever area of peace she had briefly inhabited. She levelled her eyes on me, asked

"Will you make love to me?"

I did.

Right there on the floor, under the crayon sketch. She touched the bandaged wound, asked

"Does it hurt?"

Time to be stoic, be macho, shrug it off. I said

"Like a son of a bitch."

She made love with an urgency, with a passion that was ferocious. I, as they say, went along for the ride. Afterward, she rose, and, naked, went to the fridge, took out two beers. Sam Adams, frigging Boston rules but what the hell, a cold one was just the deal. I'd already had the hot one. She uncapped them, handed me one, clinked the bottles, said

"*Sláinte.*"

What else could I say so I said it

"Good health."

She leaned over my shoulder, took down a pack of Marlboro Lights, lit two and I said

"I didn't know you smoked."

She put one between my lips, the gesture more intimate than the love making, said

"There's a lot you don't know."

Ain't that the truth? The first hits of the nicotine were magic, that rush to the blood stream, a cross between dizziness, nausea and ecstasy. Mainly, a cross, like in crucify. What I wanted was a line of coke and a double shot of bourbon so I asked

"You got any bourbon?"

She indicated a closet, said

"Top shelf."

Of course.

Self-conscious, naked, I walked to the closet, opened it. Men are no good at that casual stroll without clothes, women can pull it off with grace and us, we do it looking more than a little ridiculous. A bottle of Jim Beam and on the bottom shelf, I saw the butt of a hand gun, and the temptation to check, see it had been fired was nearly overwhelming and reading my thoughts. She said

"My dad put it there. He says a woman alone can't be too careful."

I grabbed two glasses from the sink, filled them with Beam, asked

"Water?"

"No, neat, like my man."

Okay, so it's dumb but it gave me a glow. I brought the glasses over and she had a quilt, covered us and we lay sipping the hooch, drinking the beer and imagining the world was a fine place. She asked

"What are you thinking about?"

The answer is always

"You, hon."

I was thinking *if Jeff shot me because I took his ex to dinner, what the hell would he do if he knew I'd fucked her?*

"He'd never met a cat that could tolerate him. For all he knew, his armpits gave off an unpleasant odour that only those little fuckers could smell."

—Allan Guthrie, *Two-Way Split*

I WISH I could say that after making love, sharing intimacy, we shared a depth, touching each other's souls and Shannon, she was a woman, she wanted to talk and I did the guy thing.

I slept.

Dreamt a beast was stalking me, could feel its breath on my face and came to with a shudder to find a cat, a fucking cat, staring into my eyes. I screamed. The thing took off like, well, I guess, a scalded cat. Shannon was standing at the door, mugs of steaming coffee in her hands, trying not to laugh, said

"You'll have met Byron."

I tried for some macho poise, not too easy to pull off when you've just wailed like a banshee. I blustered

"The fuck is Byron?"

She moved over, my Red Sox T-shirt emphasizing her breasts, the logo turned out. Handing me a mug, she said

"That's my other darling."

My chest hurt, my head ached and the coffee burned my tongue. I said

"I'm not fond of cats."

She wasn't fazed, said

"You're not fond of a lot of stuff, especially your own self."

Just a little too deep for me first thing on waking. I asked if I could use the shower, maybe borrow a shirt, Jeff had probably left a pile. She indicated the bathroom, said

"I ran you a bath, get you all mellowed out."

Take more than a freaking tub of hot water but I didn't share that. The bath was good and if not relaxing, it eased me down a notch. I was going to ask her about Jeff and was stalling. Checked my wound, it was raw, inflamed. My face was puffy, and I badly needed a shave. Came out, wrapped in a towel. Shannon indicated jeans, and an almost-black blue sweat shirt, said

"The jeans belonged to Jeff and the shirt is my own. And don't panic, it's the Yankees."

It was.

Tight fit but snug. Dressed, I felt marginally better and grabbed a cig, fired up, she said

"Those things will kill you."

Seemed an opening so I said

"Not if Jeff gets there first."

Her face took the direct hit, like a serious lash. She moved to the sofa, curled her feet up under her, and focused. That position, I mean, is it comfortable? I always think it's related to that yoga crap and expect a chant to walk point. She said

"Jeff has A.M.I."

All these abbreviations we have now, to skirt calling anything what it is. It's like some relation of P.M.S. I stayed standing, smoke curling above my head, like a bad omen, a useless prayer. I asked

"And that is?"

"Anger management issues."

Was she serious?

I didn't ask her but went with

"Shooting people, seems he's taking it to the next level."

A flash of anger crossed her eyes. Maybe she had some issues herself and she said

"Don't be flippant. He's the father of my child."

Gee, like I'd forgotten. I said

"How about you give me his address? I'll help him resolve some of his issues."

She took a deep breath, said

"Nicky, I like you, I like you a lot and I think I'm falling for you. But if you go after Jeff, we are done. He's the father of my child. You hurt him, where does that leave us?"

Maybe it wasn't the time to get into it, I said

"You won't tell me where he lives. I don't know what he looks like, so how am I going to do anything?"

We both let that scenario dance a little then she stood up, said

"I have to go, pick up Sean. Let me drop you at your apartment."

I said no, I'd some stuff to do and we did an awkward hug, Jeff right in there with us.

Outside, I checked up and down, damn foolish. Jeff was hardly going to show himself. I hailed a cab, had him take me to Boyle's place, time to report in.

The driver was sussing me in the mirror, asked

"Yankees fan, huh?"

Did I want to get into sports with some guy who'd be rabid in his view on how to improve the team? I said

"Naw, I borrowed the shirt."

His face showed what he thought of that and he shut down. We got to Boyle's. I overtipped and the cabbie looked pointedly at my shirt, said

"Give it back."

And was gone.

Another fine start to a day, piss off a Yankees fan. My shoulder throbbed and I dry swallowed some pain killers though I'd a feeling I'd need to mainline heroin to be numb enough for Boyle and Griffin.

I knocked on the door to the office and heard

"Yeah?"

Boyle was nose deep in the good book, Griffin reading the *Daily News.* They surveyed me, hard to read their expressions, but if I had to, I'd say Griffin was, as ever, amused. Boyle, he was just unpredictable. He closed the Bible with a slow grace, gave it a touch and then blessed himself, said

"So they shot yah?"

They?

I nodded and he indicated the chair before him and I sat. He turned to Griffin, said

"Grab us some java."

You could see that Griffin was not fond of being treated like the messenger boy but he headed out. I nearly shouted

"Yo, fellah, a cheese Danish."

Boyle lit up a cigar, took a long draw, then

"The cops been to see you?"

"Yes, sir."

The sir definitely helped. He seemed to uncoil and with his cigar, signalled for me to continue so I did.

"They asked me if I knew who did it, why anyone would want to shoot me and I gave them nothing."

Boyle smiled, said

"That's me boyo."

Griffin returned with a Starbucks tray, a mess of to-go cups on there, plunked it on the table. Boyle grabbed a grande something and Griffin had an espresso. I took the last one which was some kind of Vanilla hotchpotch. Boyle sipped, made a grimace and reached in the drawer for the Jameson. Leaned over and with out asking, poured a healthy slug into my cup. Vanilla and Irish, sounds like a hooker's special. I took a taste and it killed off the sweetness. Sometimes that's all you need. Boyle said

"Ah, that's an eye opener. So me wild colonial boy, who shot you? That Red Sox whore maybe?"

Call it reckless, but Griffin sitting there, his eyes locked on me, like some superior cobra was dancing on my nerve endings, but I went for it

"I thought Mr. Griffin might have done it."

The expression "you could have heard a pin drop" only applies if you're talking about the pin in a grenade. Griffin actually stiffened, a flash of fire in those dead eyes then Boyle laughed, loud and nasty, turned to Griffin, asked

"That true, Frankie, you shot our lad?"

Frankie?

Griffin put down his coffee, leaned over towards me, said

"I shot you, they'd be putting you in the cheap box about now."

Boyle loved that, said

"He's right, lad. Griffin only needs one shot and they don't get up but why would you think he'd shoot you? Aren't you one of our own? You are, aren't you?"

The threat was implicit and I tried for hard, said

"Mr. Griffin doesn't like me."

Boyle was having a high old time. After wiping his eyes, he finally said

"Jaysus, if Frankie shot everyone he didn't like, there wouldn't be enough hours in the day."

So, against my better judgment, I mentioned Jeff. Boyle said to Griffin

"Find out who that cunt is, cut his balls off."

I raised my hand, asked

"Mr. Boyle, I'd like to take care of this on my own tab. I think you'll understand that."

He considered it, then

"Okay, don't let it become a problem, *capisce*?"

I capisced.

He told me go home, get some rest and tomorrow, he had a new assignment for me. I was at the door when he asked

"Your old man, he take money?"

I didn't like the slur but I was in Judas mood, said

"Doesn't everyone?"

As I walked down the corridor, I could hear Boyle say

"That kid, cracks me up."

* * *

MAYBE IT WAS the crack from Boyle about my old man, or just feeling a bit lost but what the hell, I decided to go visit my parents.

Our house was quiet. Usually it was suppressed bedlam, a tension you could cut with a knife, even a blunt one. I could hear my mother in the kitchen and announced myself. She came out, wiping flour from her hands, exclaimed

"Are you alright, why aren't you still in the hospital?"

I was already sorry I came. I asked

"Where's Dad?"

She involuntarily rubbed her eye and how had I missed it at the hospital? A shiner, fading but still visible. She said

"He's staying, um, at his buddy's place for a few days."

Rage engulfed me and before I could explode she said

"He's going to AA. The drink got out of hand and when he gets his ninety days, he can come home. He's trying Nicky. Honest to God, it's a disease."

I stared at her, stated

"He hit you. The bastard hit you."

Now she was wringing her hands, dry washing them, said

"He didn't mean it. I said prayers and they were answered. He agreed to go to them meetings. Lots of his cop buddies are in it. They said he'll be fine."

Not if I could track him down first.

My mother said she'd go fix me some coffee and a bowl of porridge, keeping it Irish. The only way you can eat that shit is to douse it in Jameson. My old man, he had a work station in the garage and I headed out there, expecting to find empty bottles strewn about. Maybe I'd bag the suckers, give my mother a break.

No bottles.

In the center of the floor was a three-foot rendition of the North Tower, made of matchsticks. I moved closer and it was incredible, painstakingly constructed, and so like the real thing that I let out an impressed, "phew". It must have taken him months. I looked around and sure enough, a book of matches on the shelf. I grabbed them, approached the tower, and fired up the whole book. Let it sit on top of the edifice. The wood and sulfur caught quickly and then with a whoosh, the whole thing went up, like some damn funeral pyre.

I moved back a step and marvelled at how it burned.

Tops, four minutes, it was just a husk, smoking, and a rising smell of burnt ash. I waited a few more minutes and stared at the small mound of what used to be the North Tower then, very deliberately, I lashed out with my right foot, sending embers and ash across the floor.

Back in the kitchen, I sipped my mother's coffee, left the porridge untouched and she asked

"Is it okay?"

I waited a beat then said

"It burns."

"There was a gothic quality to the neighborhood and the cast iron colonnettes, stone gargoyles, the Italianate palaces, the ornate metal canopies, the broad-shouldered textile buildings were redolent with a sense of history I could feel and admire. And yet, there were shadows, and broken windows, razor-wire, wide cracks in the pavement, and failure and loss. And there were ghosts . . ."

—Jim Fusilli, *Closing Time*

THE NEXT WEEK, I did errands for Boyle, making drops of various packages, collecting money, and generally getting my body back in some kind of post-bullet shape. I was relying more and more on coke and that shit sneaks up on you. You come to in the morning, you have a fast hit to get you up and mobile. Then after coffee, shower, another hit to get you out the door.

I called Shannon and we had a day in the park with her little boy. I brought my old catcher's mitt. The lad and me tossed the ball around. Shannon had brought a picnic and when we sat down to have some cold cuts, French bread, a bottle of wine, she watched the boy practice with the bat. I said

"He's got an arm on him."

Her face was radiant and she said

"He likes you, likes you a lot. The truth is, I think he's a little afraid of his own father."

I was tempted to say

"Well, the guy shoots people."

But let it slide.

She added

"But you have great patience. You working at that?"

Not exactly a quality you link with a cokehead but odd thing, when I was with the kid, I didn't feel the same urge to shove the crap up my nose. I said

"No, I like being with him."

She handed me a pitcher of wine, said

"We might have something going for us."

I didn't want to spoil it by sharing my thoughts.

I was thinking of Jeff, and the guy I gave two hundred bucks to to find his address, I'd already learned his full name was Jeff Delaney and he had, as the cops say, some history, a rap sheet, one that sung consistently. Burglary, grand theft auto, robbery, aggravated assault.

A real sweetheart and this prick was walking around.

Shannon was busting my balls about maybe being a wiseguy and she had this guy in her portfolio?

Women, jeez.

We were seeing more and more of each other and it was getting real serious. I caught myself looking in jewelry stores, at engagements rings.

I was on the verge of taking the plunge when my cell rang early one morning. I'd gone to my own place as Shannon was getting Sean ready for a visit with his grandparents and she wanted one night of just the two of them. Did I feel left out? Yeah, a little.

So shoot me.

That song by Tupac, "Thugs Get Lonely Too."

The cell dragged me from a bourbon dream. I'd had me a few belts before hitting the sack. Heard Griffin go

"You up, lover boy?"

Where was the goddamned candy?

I said

"What do you want?"

He gave a mean chuckle, said

"I'm sitting in my ride outside your new flash apartment. How's that working for you?"

Fucker wanted to chat?

I found a smoke, cranked it up, still no sign of my freaking coke, snapped

"You rang me up for a chat, that it?"

More chuckling and this was not a guy who ever laughed, unless it was at a dog being tortured or other niceties. He said

"Get your arse down here. I've a wee gift for you."

I dragged on a sweat shirt, managed to brew a fast cup of java. No way I move out on any day without the caffeine hit, need that jolt, that kick start to a wasting system. Pulled on a pair of Levis and slipped my feet into a pair of Converse.

Good to go.

Oh, tousled my hair, keep that casual gig going.

Met one of the tenants on the way down. I tried

"Morning."

He glared at me. So they hadn't yet warmed to me. I added

"You have a good one."

Griffin was sitting in a black Merc, the engine running. I got in and he asked

"You didn't bring me a cup of coffee?"

I looked at him. He was wearing a black suit, to match the car I guess, and his soul. I said

"You have a rule about that stuff."

He checked his mirror, then

"Little bit of hospitality goes a long way. Didn't your parents teach you anything?"

I figured we could do this all day, so I asked

"You had something in mind, besides busting my balls?"

He reached in the dash, took out a Walther, handed it to me, said

"Take that."

Like a fool, I did.

Then he said,

"Lemme check the slide."

I handed it back. The fuck was he at?

I should have clocked his thin black leather gloves. He put the gun back in the dash, said

"Excellent."

I asked

"What's going on?"

He reached in his jacket, pulled out a .38, levelled it at me and I shouted

"You're here to show me your fucking gun collection? It's lovely, now what the hell is going on?"

The gun still steady on my chest, he said

"Jeff Delaney. Got his own fool self shot to death this morning, early hours I believe and guess what the caliber of weapon is?"

The Walther.

He smiled, said

"With your fine set of pristine prints. Now get out of the car."

I didn't move, asked

"You're setting me up to take the fall for his murder?"

He sighed as if to ask, *how dumb are you?* Said

"Only if you don't do what we ask."

"Do the fuck what?"

"Kill the cop."

* * *

MY MIND WAS on fire. Jeff was dead, my fingerprints on the pistol, and my ass in the frame if I didn't off Todd. I did some coke, tried to get my head straight or at least functioning. I was going to run, that was for damn sure. I had some cash, well, plenty of cash, and if I headed to some obscure burg, laid low, maybe Todd and his blue buddies would take down Boyle and Griffin.

But Shannon, if I took off, Griffin would use her for leverage to get me back. I shouted

"Ah, fuck."

Didn't help.

Try this: I waste Todd.

Wouldn't fly, not even for a nano second. He was my buddy, my brother. I called him said

"I'm in deep shit, I need help."

He was quiet then said

"You've always been in deep shit but needing help, that's new."

I needed a lecture now?

I snapped

"You gonna help or not?"

He was.

We met at a diner on 6th and 33rd. I love diners but that day, I wanted a bar, and lots of drinks. Todd was calling the shots, no pun intended, so the goddamn diner it was. He was wearing the battered leather and yeah, Red Sox cap. I asked

"You have to shove it in my face every time?"

He gave me a hurt look, unusual for him, then picked up the menu, said

"Eggs over easy, you think?"

I had a flask, lethal with Beam, used it to jolt my coffee. Todd said

"That will help, keep you clear headed."

Before I could reply, he said

"Your girl's husband was shot to death last night. I'm guessing it wasn't you. Tell me I'm right. You did that, even I can't help you."

I shook my head and he said

"Lemme guess. Griffin. And they've got you framed. And to get out, you have to waste me?"

Impressed the hell out of me. He smiled, said

"I'm very good at being a cop, Nicky."

I gave it up, tired all of a sudden, asked

"What am I going to do?"

He reached in his pocket, took out a sheaf of papers, said

"There's a small town in Kentucky, I've got a buddy there. He'll give you a job. Lie real low and we'll take care of things this end. There's a ticket in there for Penn Station. You leave tomorrow morning."

It was too fast. I had a hundred questions, but went for one

"What about Shannon?"

"I'll talk to her. You just get the hell out. Things are going down. You're only a nuisance now. We'll bring you back for the indictments."

I went

"You want me to testify?"

He signalled the waitress, said

"You've got a choice?"

He was ordering the eggs. My mind was in a tailspin. "Leave the city?"

He nodded, said

"It'll be okay. Messy but I'll sort it out."

I wish I could have believed him, asked

"What about my parents?"

"Go see them tonight, tell them you're going for a fresh start. They'll be glad you're shaping up."

Bollocks.

His eggs came and he dug in. My coffee was cold and not even the Beam could liven it. I asked

"That's it, I just split and what, wait?"

His mouth full, he said

"You got it. You're out of it."

I stood up, threw a mess of bucks on the table, said

"I'll be moving then. Any last words of advice, any wisdom to speed me on my way?"

I let the sarcasm leak all over the words. He said

"Sure, you should have had the eggs. They're real fine."

That evening I called Shannon and her opening words were

"You murdering bastard."

I tried to explain but she was shouting, calling me all sorts of names. I managed to say

"I have to leave town but Todd will be by. You'll see, I'm not the one who killed Jeff."

She was quiet and I thought maybe I'd reached her, then she said

"Run, it's what I'd expect of you."

And hung up.

I had one item of business to take care of. Todd might have his plans but I had to do something. I called Griffin, told him I'd decided to do as he asked but I needed him to help me dispose of the body. He said

"Atta boy."

"The pier, you know which one."

Deserted at night, used to be one busy mother but not no more. Only the vermin run it now, human and rodent. I was parked by the water when Griffin drove up. His smirk in place, he got out of the car, slid in beside me, asked

"So, when are you doing the dirty deed?"

I said

"It's done."

He was surprised, took a moment then,

"The bold policeman, where's he at?"

"In the trunk."

Before he could digest this I shot him in the gut, twice. His eyes were wide and I said

"They say that hurts like a son of a bitch. Are they right?"

I thought about putting the third one between his eyes, but that was too easy, not enough suffering.

Dropping him over the pier, I said

"May you rot in hell."

*   *   *

THE NEXT MORNING, I still had the Buick and drove by the North Tower, parked for a moment. I still had time to go up there, reconcile with my old man. I gave it serious consideration then let out a long breath, said

"Fuck him."

Turned the car, headed for Penn Station. I was thinking of Shannon and hoped someone would still teach Sean how to catch. That kid had an arm on him.

My eyes were watering, probably the coke.

I hoped I could hook up in Kentucky. I mean, they have some good ole boys there.

You think?

TODD

"When two people fall in love and begin to feel that they're made for one another, then it's time for them to break off, for by going on they have everything to lose and nothing to gain."

—Søren Kierkegaard

MEN AREN'T SUPPOSED to say shit like this, but the fact is that I loved Nicky. Yeah, here's the part where I'm supposed to say, I wasn't *in love* with Nicky. Sorry to disappoint you. I was *in love* with him, not like lustfully in love with him. Didn't want to have his babies or anything, not that I could differentiate in third grade. We don't talk about it much in our culture, but there's very little can hold a candle to the infatuation a young boy has for his first hero. For some boys, it's their dads. My dad . . . yeah, right!

Nick, he hated his father for the way he'd smack him around. I was jealous. At least his dad gave a shit, if not for Nick, for something, anyway. And the rough treatment produced in Nick another quality I admired: rage. We all have anger. I have more than most, but Nick was different. He was a rage cheetah, zero to seventy in the beat of a heart. It wasn't blind rage either, though he was sometimes blinded by it. He could focus it like a laser sight on the forehead of his next target.

What's that blues song, "Born Under a Bad Sign"? If it wasn't for bad luck, I think the lyrics go, I'd have no luck at all. If it wasn't for rage, sometimes I think Nicky would have no feelings at all. Everything—friendship, grief, even love— seemed to be a permutation of his rage. Only later did I come to the realization that it wasn't all his father's doing. Nick had the rage in him like my mom had the sadness in her, on the molecular level.

Guess I should have seen it when we were kids. There was this one time we were playing stickball on the street and Vinny Podesta, the block bully, knocked me down to get to a ball. What an asshole Vinny was. I mean, we were on the same fucking team and he knocked me over just because he could. Nicky like exploded. He broke Vinny's nose, climbed on top of him and just started smacking him with the back of his hand and I mean hard. Never seen anything like it. None of us kids had.

Yeah, we'd all had street fights. Came with the territory. You live in the rain forest, you get wet. So the thing about most street fights, especially among kids, is that they're pretty ritualized. They have a form. It's like when you see two rams butting heads. Before they get to it, there's gesturing, threat behavior, each combatant giving the other a chance to back down. Watch the next time you see a bunch of boys in a schoolyard. There's name calling, screaming, then a push. The push is the last chance for backing off. If there's a push back, the fight's coming. If the kid that gets pushed reverts to name calling, the fight's been averted. That wasn't Nick's way.

You even looked at Nick the wrong way, he was coming for you. And it's not like he started off easy and gave you a chance for retreat. No, it was all out from the first punch. Nicky didn't lose many fights. That was the thing, he had rage. There was this other time, when we were older. We'd been smoking a few doobs and drinking in a trendy Park Slope hole. The bathroom was like the deli counter at Waldbaums: you needed to get a number. Went out to the alley to piss.

Found some mook trying to force himself on this girl, had her by the hair, face pressed to the brick wall, and was tearing at her panties from her lifted skirt. Kicked the ever living crap out of him. Pounded his face. Nicky, man, kicked at him like a mule. Wouldn't stop. Kept swinging his boot, kicking and stomping. Even the chick we saved was freaked out.

"Whoa, whoa, Nicky," I said, bear-hugging him and pulling him away. "You've got to rein it in, bro."

"Why?" was all he said.

Things changed for us forever after that night. Even when Nick did his six months in Spofford, a place that would put the devil into a martyr, he was more in control. He really seemed on the edge. Of what, I couldn't say, but it was nothing good.

The rest of my life changed in short order.

Been working at the airport for my Uncle Harry for a few years out of high school. Could have gone to college, should have, but I didn't have the heart for more clueless teachers with advanced degrees in irrelevance. My mom was too self-absorbed to protest. I'm sure my dad was disappointed—hell, name me someone or something that didn't disappoint him—but he wouldn't have had the stones to say boo. Think maybe if he had said something, I would have gone for him. Of course, he didn't. Why fuck up a perfect losing streak?

Uncle Harry was a fucking charmer, a real class act. Brought a smoking blonde half his age to my cousin Jay's bar mitzvah. She knew Harry for the low rent asshole he was. Caught her sucking the drummer's cock during a band break. Saw me watching. Stared at me. It was like a dare. Grow up in Brooklyn, you recognize a dare. "Go ahead, tell that fat fuck!" her eyes seemed to say. I didn't say a word.

Anyway, the cargo area at the airport was the Wild West with jets. It was its own fucking little world with its own codes and rules. First thing you learned was that the Port Authority of New York and New Jersey had about as much control of the cargo area as a bull rider has of the bull. The Mob ran the unions and the truckers and the container stations and the warehouses. If you farted near JFK, the Boys got their ten percent.

The low level guys ate their lunches at The Owl. The Owl was a real upscale joint, showed porn movies at the bar during lunch, but they did serve great eggplant parm heroes. The Boys on the next level up fucked their whores at the Jade East Motor Inn on the South Conduit. That's where Harry had met the blonde cocksucker he'd taken to my cousin Jay's. You gotta love Uncle Harry, a real class act, but the blonde was right about him, he was smalltime. It was that you had to be in that world to know it. To the Boys, Harry was the fat Jew they tolerated because he earned for them.

That was another thing you learned quick. There was no such thing as friends among thieves. These guys would pat you on the back, drink with you, slip you a c-note every now and then, but it was meaningless. They were cold bastards, but the guineas were sweethearts as compared to the donkeys. Christ, the Irish were real fuckers. At least with the Italians, you knew most of their decisions were based on earning. You had some sense of where you stood with them boys. Was different with the boyos. They strayed from logic a bit too often to suit me. Then again I've always been a bit of a moth. Show me the flame and I'm there.

Met Boyle and Griffin through Harry, and Nick met Boyle through me. Harry had all of Boyle's import/export brokerage. Not that I knew or cared what was in the boxes I trucked back and forth from the City to the warehouse at JFK and back again. It was Boyle who offered me my first real money for my first real crime. Initially it was just driving, then we moved onto "other" things: nothing violent, but always with the rush of potential violence. Never knew when someone would walk in when they weren't supposed to. Boyle, the Bible-thumping hypocrite, had his own imported boyo to do his violence.

Griffin had the real brogue, not the second generation cartoon bullshit that came outta Boyle's gob. Not that Griffin talked much. A quiet fucker, he spoke with his fists and pistols, a knife too, if need be. Griffin had the real troubles in him, too. He'd been with the Provos, it was whispered, whoever the hell they were. I knew about the IRA, what did I know from Provos and Protestants? Did I give a shit who wore orange and who wore green and who marched through what neighborhood? Truth be told, Jews took guilty pleasure at the concept of Christians at each other's throats. Guilty pleasure's the only kind we know. Kept my eye on Griffin even when Boyle spoke. The level of Boyle's danger reached only as deep as Griffin's darkness. That made Mr. Boyle pretty fucking dangerous. I'd seen some of Griffin's handiwork.

Only once he confided in me was after a particularly brutal job. Guy owned a few hot dog trucks owed Boyle several large and was slow to pay. Big mistake being a late payer. Watched Griffin snap every one of the man's fingers like they were popsicle sticks. Stopped getting nauseous when he switched to his left hand.

"How do you do it?"

Griffin knew what I meant.

"Violence is violence done for whatever cause. You blow up a car in Derry or you snap some tardy fooker's fingers, it's violence. Don't somehow think the Lord keeps two sets of ledgers. You cross the line, you cross the line."

Such was the extent of his philosophy.

Suppose I was moving up the ladder and I'd gotten Nick some work with me, mostly petty shit, but then Nick discovered he had a talent for boosting cars. He made Boyle and a lot of Third World bastards happy. Then something happened to put a crimp in my career. My mom exercised her prerogative.

"The heart shuts,
The sea slides back,
The mirrors are sheeted."
                    —Sylvia Plath, from her poem "Contusion"

IF THE IRISH have a heart for anything, it's death. Since
sorrow is their stock and trade, a mother's death is like a
fucking grand slam in the bottom of the ninth. And suicide?
Holy hell, you add a sin like that to the equation and it's epic.
Boyle quoted to me from the good book, patted me on the
back, and told me to take all the time I needed. Like he was
a magnanimous fellow looking out for my well being. Yeah,
sure. It was that Nick and his cars were pulling in some
serious cash. And besides, Nick was one of their own.

No, it was Griffin's reaction that shocked me. He
actually displayed a bit of humanity, as far as it went. Shook
my hand and said, "Sorry for your troubles." Gave me a
smirk. Was as close to real sympathy as he was ever going to
get. Proved the authenticity of Irish-ness I suppose and that
even killers had mothers once, too.

When I got the call from my dad, I was in a bit of shock.
It's not like I didn't know the call would come someday.
That my mother would eventually kill herself was as much a
surprise as sunset. The surprise was that she had lasted *this*
long. Think even my mom's shrinks knew they were simply
delaying the inevitable. She was broken inside. All the
king's horses and all the king's lithium couldn't put Sophie
back together again.

Have to hand it to her, though. She did it with flare,
with a gesture, a final *fuck you!* to all the other mothers on
the old block. Sophie may have been too haunted to love her
son or husband or to care about the whispers and stares, but
that was not to say she didn't notice or didn't hear. So when

she stepped out of bed sometime in the middle of the night, went to the broom closet to retrieve the step ladder and nylon rope—the rope having already been cut to length and formed into a crude noose—climbed to the top rung of the squat ladder, slung and secured the rope over the fat low limb of the old oak in front of our stoop, snugged the noose tight around her neck, and kicked the ladder away, Sophie was paying back her neighbors in full. It made me want to applaud. She had achieved in death something she had failed at in life; I was proud of her.

When I got past the shock, I was pretty fucking relieved. It's a cruel thing to say, true or not. But she robbed me. Even more surprising than Griffin's reaction was my dad's. Cried! He cried over her. This woman, this un-wife, this un-mother, this stranger who had filled up his emptiness with her own miserable existence, this is who he shed tears for! Didn't think it was possible for him to shrink any further and yet he did.

Her funeral at Rosenzweig's on Coney Island Avenue and Avenue M was about as well attended as a 1977 Mets game. The rabbi had to ask people to move up and fill in the empty seats. Of the neighbors, only Nick's mom came. Given Sophie's parting love letter to the block, can't say that I expected a big show of support. Nicky was there too as was Uncle Harry, cousin Ira the cop and Sheila his wife. Harry, at least, had the rare good taste to leave his latest cocksucker back at the Jade East. And as the service was conducted by a rent-a-rabbi, things moved along apace.

The burial was out on Long Island along an avenue they might as well have called Cemetery Street or Burial Boulevard. There was like ten different graveyards for Jews, Catholics, Lutherans, veterans, you name it. Think I might have seen one for clowns and other deceased circus performers. Wondered if they buried clowns in little cars, ten to a car. It was all such a bunch of crap or, as Boyle might say, a load a shite. What does any of it matter to the dead?

Clearly the rabbi had received the going flat rate for his services as he picked up the speed with which he rendered his graveside ceremony. Spoke so quickly the words blended together into a kind of buzzing. When he was done, the few of us there tossed some spadefuls of dirt atop Sophie's coffin. That was that. My dad didn't even bother asking if I wanted to sit *shiva* with him. If I said no, he would've been forced to back down. So why bother?

As I walked away from the gravesite to the one pitiful limo, cousin Ira hooked his arm through mine. In my family this was a major sign of affection.

"Does this mean we're engaged?" I asked.

"Just keep your mouth shut, wiseguy, and keep walking."

"But the limo, my dad . . ."

"I'll drive Todd home," he called to my father, waving him to go on ahead.

We stopped until the limo and the two or three other cars pulled away. I remember the sick look on my Uncle Harry's face when he saw me. Thought he might actually have been sad his sister hung herself, naked on the tree in front of her house, shit and piss running down her cold, bare legs. No, not Harry. He got into his black El Dorado and sped away, the front tires spitting gravel back in defiance.

When I tried removing my arm from Ira's grip, he squeezed my hand till it nearly broke.

"Come on, asshole, someone wants to meet you."

Ira was my mom's cousin and as popular as a lungful of cancer. At that infamous bar mitzvah of my cousin Jay's, people lined up to talk to Harry like he was the Pope. No one talked to Ira. No one ever talked to Ira. Jews are funny that way. They respect the law, but not those who enforce it. Ira was a joyless fuck. A good detective by all measures, but joyless.

He marched me to a stone bench in front of a row of four graves. A black granite headstone marked each of the graves. Each bore the name Einstein. Was there like a message in that, I wondered?

Standing by the bench was a hulk of a man with a shaven head and thick neck. It was the kind of neck with ripples in the back. He wore an ill-fitting gray suit that might as well have had SEARS CLOSEOUT embroidered down the sleeves. But he was shaped so that even a Sayville Row suit would have looked like a Halloween costume on him. *Cop*! *Cop*! *Cop*! The alarm bells rang in my head.

"This is Captain O'Connor," Ira said.

"Christ, another donkey."

Cousin Ira unhinged his arm, gave me a quick jab in my left kidney that left me on my knees and gagging on Sonya Einstein's grave.

O'Connor crossed himself—you just gotta love the fucking Irish—knelt down beside me and said, "Pleasure to meet you, too. Sorry for your troubles."

His smirk was broader than Griffin's but had the same chilling effect. This guy meant business.

"You and me, Todd, we're gonna be great friends," he continued, his sour breath making me cringe. He held his left hand out to me. "Come on, lad, take it. It's gonna be yours in a coupl'a months anyways."

I looked back and saw Ira was fully prepared to administer his unique form of renal massage to my other kidney if I didn't follow instructions. I held out my left hand. In it, O'Connor placed a NYPD detective's shield.

"What the f—"

Ira landed his punch before I could get the *–uck* out of my mouth. Now I coughed up my breakfast onto Sonya's grave.

"Jesus and his blessed mother!" O'Connor exclaimed in much the same way as Boyle might. "Show some respect for the dead."

Managed to right myself and make it to the bench. O'Connor took the seat beside me.

"Now here's the offer, lad. You'll be one of us or you'll be one of them," he said, pointing to the Einsteins. "It's a simple choice. I run the OCCB—do you know what that is, son?"

"Organized Crime Control Bureau."

"Smart boy." O'Connor patted my cheek. "As I was saying, I run the OCCB Task Force that oversees criminal enterprises where more than one gang of scumbags does business with another. You know, like how the wops and sheenies at JFK make nice with those shanty pricks you work for."

"I don't work for anyone but my Uncle—"

O'Connor slapped my face hard.

"Don't take that attitude with me, lad. That fat cunt you call your uncle has been in my pocket for five years. So maybe when the boyos cut his heart out and feed it to him, they can lay him beside you."

"Harry's been an informant for years," Ira chimed in. "And one way or another, he's a dead man."

"That's right, Todd, your uncle's fucked. But for you, there's a chance."

I held the shield up. "You call this a chance?"

"No, lad, I call it an *only* chance. And you're lucky to have it. How you've managed all these years to avoid arrest is beyond me. Had you been arrested, let alone convicted of anything, you'd be fucked as well."

"How's that?"

"Because we'd be hard pressed to get you on the job with a record, shithead," Ira said. "So we're making this an elevator ride for you."

"Pretty cryptic for a cop, cuz."

"Then let me explain it to you. You're one of us or one of them. It's up or down with no change of direction."

"What if I choose them?"

"It's your prerogative, I suppose," O'Connor admitted. "But then you'd be the second person in your family to commit suicide."

"Suicide?"

"Exactly so," O'Connor said. "Cause even if you don't take the offer, we'll let it leak that you're working for us and you'll be dead."

"That's murder, not suicide."

"You're splitting hairs, lad. Either way, you'll be dead."

"Nice operation you guys are running," I sneered.

"You think that stone cold Griffin would give you an option? Come on, lad, use that—what's that expression, Ira—your *Yiddisher. . .*"

"*Yiddisher kupf,*" Ira said. "Jewish head."

"Yes, your Jewish smarts," O'Connor translated.

Wasn't being left with much of a choice. Nicky would've told them both to go fuck themselves and taken a swing at O'Connor. I wasn't Nicky.

"I'll do it."

"Decisive, I like that," O'Connor said, beaming like a new father. "Done at the speed of light. Appropriate, given our proximity."

Somebody was bound to make an Einstein joke. Glad it wasn't me.

"Do you like cheese steaks, Detective Rosen?"

"Yeah, why?"

"Ira will explain it to you on the ride back to your father's house. Welcome aboard." O'Connor patted my back. He knew I wasn't about to shake his hand. He did, however, hold his left hand out to me. "The shield, son. You'll have to earn it."

Tossed it in my own puke and walked toward Ira's car. Heard O'Connor laughing as I walked away.

"I have heard the mermaids singing, each to each.
I do not think they will sing to me."
—T.S. Eliot, from his poem, "The Love Song of J. Alfred
Prufrock"

COVER STORY. COVER girl. Women are the perfect camouflage. You could have thought up a thousand elaborate excuses for why I had to leave Brooklyn, why I had to quit Uncle Harry's, why I had to temporarily part company with Boyle and the boyos, yet none would have done the trick like the mention of a woman. Let me tell you something, it's men that are the bigger suckers for love. Women look for love. Men look for pussy and stumble onto love. And Christ, when we stumble it's an endless fall. Who do you think misses their first loves more, men or women? If you say women, you're a fool.

So when I went to Boyle and told him I'd met someone and that I was moving to Philadelphia to be with her, he didn't flinch. Fuck, not only didn't he flinch, the man offered to get me in with some donkeys down Broad Street way. Politely refused, saying that if I was going to do dirt, it would only be on his behalf. Smiled like a proud father. Unnerved me, that smile. Never seen its like from my own dad. With the atmosphere surrounding my mom's suicide and with Nicky earning like he was, Boyle didn't give my leaving a second thought. Still O'Connor and Ira thought we should make a bit of a show of it, wanted to prove to Boyle's crew that there was a girl and that I was smitten.

Didn't have to pretend, for I *was* smitten, immediately, on the spot, even now. Met at a Starbucks up in Scarsdale: a town of well-to-do Asians and Jews pretending to be Biff and Muffy at the club. Not the kind of place you'd be apt to find

Boyle, Griffin or Nicky sipping Pinot Noir by the pool or quietly clapping by the tee box and shouting, "Well struck!"

"You Rosen?" she asked, coming up behind me.

"Last time I checked." I made to stand.

"Don't bother. I'm Velez, Leeza Velez."

God, just thinking about the first time I saw her gives me that odd sensation, a cross between nerves and nirvana. She was about five foot five with elegant curves, straight sable hair that hung just slightly over her shoulders. She had bright brown eyes, a nose and jaw line that plastic surgeons could only hope to reproduce, and a dangerous mouth. Her teeth were even and white, her lips plush but not extravagant. The combination made for an electric smile, make believe though it was.

"Kiss me!"

"What?"

"We're in love, remember?"

Kissed her awkwardly, like I had a mouth full of braces. Felt about twelve years old.

"Christ, you'll have to do better than that," she said. "If we're being watched, they're gonna think you're either a liar or half a fag."

So I folded her in my arms and kissed her hard on the mouth, my tongue slipping effortlessly between her lips. If she was surprised or displeased, she didn't show it. Didn't have to see her in workout clothes to know she was well muscled and strong. Could feel her power. When I pulled back, noticed that in spite of her name, dark skin and vaguely Hispanic features, there was another kind of mojo at work in her.

"Puerto Rican, but not one hundred percent," I said.

"You taste my kiss and tell me the percentage of spic in my blood? It's blood, asshole, not red wine."

"Am I right or what?"

"We're all mongrels in this country. It makes for beauty and barbarity."

"A philosopher."

"A U.S. Marshal. I'm here to keep you safe and watch your ass, not kiss it. I'm not here to suck your dick or wash your clothes," she said, all the time smiling. "Do we understand one another?"

Smiled back with no pretense. Held my fingers a few inches apart. "So I'm sure you have a file on me this thick, but I don't know anything about you."

"What you wanna know?"

"Puerto Rican and . . . ?"

"This shit again!" Caught a glimmer of mischief in her eye. "Guess!"

"Irish."

"Yeah, some of that."

"Russian."

"Some of that, too."

"Anything else?" I asked.

"Probably."

"If this is an NYPD gig, why is a U.S. Marshal involved?"

"Cooperation between agencies."

"Bullshit! Even subway fare jumpers know the Feds and the NYPD cooperate about as well as hyenas and lions. You guys must be getting something out of it."

"We think Griffin killed one of our witnesses," she said. "We don't stand for that."

Bought us some coffees and she told me how things were going to work. This wasn't a debate or a negotiation. This was give and take. She gave. I took. She talked. I shut up.

She'd already set us up in an apartment in Philadelphia over by the University of Pennsylvania. It wasn't the greatest neighborhood, but it was one that would be within our means. We would tell the world that she worked as an administrative assistant in the bursar's office. When we'd decided to move in together, she had gotten me a job with the university as a maintenance man and I'd had to undergo a few weeks of training before I could take the job.

"How'd we meet?" I snuck in a question as she inhaled.

"Don't volunteer to explain, makes you look guilty. Anyone asks, and only if they ask, we met in a bar in Sheepshead Bay while I was visiting a girlfriend I went to Brooklyn College with. Don't get more detailed than that. Anymore questions?"

"Will you marry me?"

Can't imagine a bullet would have stunned her more. Her face went blank, but she recovered quickly. "Fuck off," she said. "I'll see you tonight."

She kissed me again. This time, it was Leeza Velez kissing like the awkward twelve-year old.

* * *

AXEL'S ON FLATBUSH Avenue was Nicky's idea. It was a neighborhood bar about as trendy as a heart attack. Don't think they'd updated the place since that cocksucker O'Malley had moved the Dodgers. You had to hand it to Nicky; he wasn't letting the first money, or, serious wedge, as Boyle might call it, affect him. He was just another Brooklyn asshole. Rage kept him grounded.

Had picked Velez up at the D train stop at Flatbush and Dekalb, kissed her when she got into the car. This time neither of us kissed like a child. We'd gotten past that one bit of awkwardness. Still, she was acting the part. Enjoyed the performance.

"Yes or no?" I asked.

"Yes or no what?"

"It's only right, you know, when a guy proposes . . ."

She ignored that. "Tell me a story about you and Nick."

"You must have a file—"

"No stories in the file."

Told her about Vinny Podesta and stickball.

Leeza wasn't Nick's type. Well, to fuck maybe, but not to love. Had trouble picturing her not being anyone's type. And not that I could wager on it, but I didn't figure thieving boyos were exactly up her alley. Then why the fuck was I sick with jealousy at watching Leeza and Nick shoot a game of Eight Ball? For fuck's sake, was this what pure rage was like? If it was, then God had put his finger on my shoulder. Knowledge was revealed.

Rage got me as high as I'd ever been. It was coke and crystal meth cooked until it turned black and thick as breakfast syrup. *Excuse me, waiter, can I have some rage for my pancakes?* Christ, I tell you I could have killed them both and myself in that brief second. Saw in that moment that I was both my mom and dad; so empty that I would kill for a woman who was in all ways but her kiss, a stranger; so full of pain I wanted to do it. Drank my Sam Adams instead. On the whole, a better idea.

"Watch out for that one," Nicky said, coming back to the bar for another round.

My heart jumped into my throat, but I managed a question. "How so?"

"She loves you. Love's trouble."

My heart found its way back into my chest. Nick needed to stick to rage and hot wiring cars. Clearly, he was no expert on the subject of love.

"It's a little late for that, Nicky."

"You're fucked."

Didn't I know it?

A devilish, crooked smiled cracked his face.

"What's up with you?" I asked.

"You told her about how I kicked the shit outta Vinny P., huh?"

"Had to tell her something good about you and it was the only thing I could think of."

"Nice."

"I try."

"You ever think about Vinny P.?" Nick wondered. "I do sometimes."

"Probably in Elmira doing a ten-year bid and taking it up the ass for cigarette money."

"Hope he knows smoking's bad for his health."

"Imagine what we'd be saying about him if we really didn't like him."

Nick patted my cheek. "Fuck Vinny Podesta! I'm gonna miss you, bro."

"Me too."

"Okay," he said. "Time to get back there and get my ass kicked again by your girlfriend."

"And as I watched I felt, quite suddenly, as bleak and lonely as I had in a long time. Maybe it was because I was still half asleep, or maybe it was the fading light that brought it on. Or maybe it was that, even watching her familiar ritual of dressing and departure, Clare seemed utterly a stranger."

—Peter Spiegelman, *Black Maps*

I GOT TRAINING all right, but it had little to do with picking up stray papers with a pointy stick. During my time in Philadelphia, don't think I once set foot on the university campus. Ask me the school's colors and I couldn't tell you. My waking hours were consumed by two things: learning to be a cop and convincing Leeza Velez I was worth loving. Even now I'm not sure how successful I was at either.

Every day, bag lunch in hand, I left our third-floor walkup at 6:15 AM. Dressed in my green coveralls and steel-toed work boots, I'd start walking to the campus and turn down an alley. There I'd climb into the back of a work van that had been booty from a drug seizure and off I went. It was an odd life, one layer of façade atop another layer of bullshit, covering a charade. But hey, if the vacuum of my parents' lives had prepared me for anything, it was this: It's hard to lose yourself when you don't know who the fuck you are to begin with.

What was different for me was that I was on the accelerated plan. My training began the minute I got into the van and didn't stop until the van dropped me off at 6:00 PM. Took some classes at the Philadelphia Police Academy and had private classes with cops from Philly and NYPD instructors. Sometimes I felt like a guy with a funnel down his throat. These guys were shoving food down as fast as they could and it was all I could do not to choke. Think I absorbed it more than learned it.

Only part I enjoyed was my weapons training. It wasn't like I hadn't carried for years, but I never really knew what the hell I was doing. You buy a Glock on the street, guy doesn't offer to teach you how to use it. *Man, think of it like one of them idiot-proof cameras, aim and shoot. Lens cap's like the safety. Don't forget to take it off. You hear what I'm sayin'?* Was encouraged to spend hours on the range. Got proficient with a 9mm. I was fucking magic with a .38, felt like an extension of myself.

No one ever told me to imagine the paper target as someone I hated. Did that all on my own. One day it was Boyle, the next day Griffin. My favorite target was O'Connor. I'd imagine him calling me lad or son and I'd start pumping slugs into where his fat neck rolls would have been.

About a month into my cram course, started doing ride-alongs in patrol cars, one or two nights a week. I was strictly forbidden to participate. Was there to watch and learn. It was during this time I met a skell who'd raped his sister and killed her friend. What a twisted piece of shit. Told me his folks had both died of cancer. As if I gave a rat's ass. Was the cancer, he claimed, that had wrecked his head.

"How's that, scumbag?"

"It's coming for me, the cancer, man. At night, I can't sleep cause I hear the clock ticking, the cancer clock."

Like that explained it all. Like that explained anything.

Meanwhile, Leeza Velez and I settled into this parallel universe existence. We lived separate lives together. Made it really clear that she wasn't interested in discussing her life with me and was less interested in discussing mine, that as long as the world bought our act and I kept drawing breath, it met her expectations. I was less satisfied with the arrangement, though there was little I could do about it.

The one reprieve I got from life behind the invisible partition came on Friday and Saturday nights. Maintenance work wasn't rocket science and no one would buy that I had to stay in on weekends cramming for my exams on leaf raking. And since our cover was that we were in love, we had to go out and act the parts. Bar scene in Philly was fun and several-fold less pretentious than Manhattan's. Although Velez steadfastly refused to share any details of her life beyond the limits of her current assignment, she was more willing to let me talk about growing up in Brooklyn, about my folks, about Nicky and the old block. She even laughed sometimes when I'd tell her about the shit Nicky and me used to pull.

As the weeks passed, stuff happened, small signs of thawing that went barely noticed. She'd catch me staring at her and she would take an extra beat to turn away. We'd reach for the same section of the paper and our fingers would brush, linger. Pure fucking electricity for me. Indifferent expression from her. All quickly forgotten. Took her once folding my laundry as a declaration of love. A man looking for signs can find 'em anywhere.

Then there was the kissing. It's strange, kissing her had become everything to me. Can't explain it, but her lips touching mine had become more meaningful for me than any full blown sex I'd ever had and I'd had plenty. During the week when my instructors would begin to drone on, often found myself daydreaming about holding her in my arms, the feel of her cheeks against my palms, the taste of beer on her tongue. Eventually, it stopped mattering to me that none of it mattered to her.

One Friday night her cell phone rang just as we were headed out the door. She picked up. She barely spoke, nodded her head a few times, hung up. Knew better than to ask. Asked anyway. Got no answer. No shock there, yet something had changed. Her body language was different. The awkwardness to the kissing had returned. She was very distracted and apologized several times for asking me to repeat myself.

When we got back to the apartment, Leeza Velez, U.S. Marshal headed straight into her room. Didn't think anything of it. Had grown accustomed to being shut out the second the front door shut behind us. But as I lay half asleep on the futon in the dark, my head digesting some bit of info my instructors had fed me during the past month, I heard her. Velez was sobbing. Tried to ignore it. Sure. Couldn't. Shuffled down the hallway to the bedroom.

"Hey, Velez, you okay?"

"Come in."

Leeza was standing naked next to the bed, her body backlit by the dim bulb of a small reading lamp. Her body was everything I had imagined it to be. She was muscular and well defined without distracting rips and cuts. Her muscles curved and sloped, making smooth transitions from one to the next. Her nipples were hard and larger than I'd envisioned. Her breasts were on the small side, but round and free from the pull of gravity. Her legs were like a sculptor's idea of perfection: taut, lean, long, curved. It took more than near darkness to hide beauty.

When I moved my lips to ask, she pressed her index finger across my mouth.

"Sssshhhhhh."

It was more a plea than a command. Leeza knelt down and took me fully into her mouth. From that second on, kisses weren't ever going to be enough.

* * *

WHEN I ROLLED over the next morning, Leeza's side of the bed was cold. And when I opened my eyes, O'Connor was staring back at me.

"Morning, lad," he said as plainly as if this was how he started all his Saturdays. "Don't bother looking for her. Seems you two have broken up. Pity that."

"What?" I asked though I'd heard him perfectly well. And when I scanned the room, I could see that any trace of Leeza Velez had been removed.

"You've done well, son. Time to move on."

"Move on where?"

"Southie, South Boston."

"But—"

"Get packed, probie," he said. "You've got a week back home before you head to Beantown. It's there you'll learn to be a man. I'll get us some coffees while you shower up."

After O'Connor left, I hesitated. Could still taste Leeza on my lips and smell her scent in the air. Showered, removing more traces of Velez, but not all. Have to scrub my soul for that.

"In the house of the hangman
do not talk of rope"
—Stanley Moss, from his poem "The Hangman's Love Song"

I WAS A zombie.

Before Philly, I may not have had a firm handle on who Todd Rosen was, exactly. No, I was dead inside. Not dead, exactly. The dead can't feel the hurt the way I can. No, was like one of those patients on the operating table who wakes up in the middle of their surgery unable to move, but exquisitely aware of the scalpel. Christ, wished the doctor'd just cut my throat and gotten it over with.

It was impossible for me to believe how deeply I'd entwined Leeza Velez into the fabric of myself. Fucking crazy that I could feel so utterly emptied and alone over a woman who'd shared herself with me for a solitary night. For all I knew Leeza Velez wasn't her name. Maybe that was it. Her distance had let me create a life for us, a life for her not only that didn't exist, but would never, could never exist. All of it woven out of a dangerous smile, brown skin, and meaningless kisses.

Brooklyn, Nicky, my dad were strangers to me, worse than strangers. Guess that's what O'Connor wanted: vertigo, discomfort, disorientation. Had never been so off balance in my life. Sidewalks where Nicky and I had scratched our initials in wet cement with a stick, seemed foreign to me now. For fuck's sake, I was foreign to my own self.

It was Axel's again. Nicky's idea, of course. Said it was fine when he asked if that suited me. What did it matter? Once pain hits a certain threshold, you might as well see how much you can take. And man, I was like a flashing neon sign, alternating between deadness and the pain. On. Off. On. Off. On . . . But it was more than Leeza. It was what

I'd become, what I'd let myself be turned into. Looked at myself in the mirror behind the bar. Christ, I thought, a cop, a fucking cop!

Nicky threw his arm over my shoulder, kissed me on the cheek. "C'mon, Todd, drink your beer and cheer up."

"You ever meet anybody that cheered up on demand?"

"Griffin."

We both had a laugh at that. Didn't last long.

"Jesus, pal, I never seen you like this. Wanna talk about it?"

"What's to talk, Nick? She walked out on me."

"Did you see it coming?" he asked.

"Maybe. Guess I didn't really know her."

"Who knows any woman?"

Wasn't inclined to argue.

He checked his watch. It was getting close to ten. On O'Connor's orders I'd ask to meet with Boyle. Nick had made the arrangements. Shrugged his head that we better get moving. Stood with my beer glass in hand, prepared to chug the rest, when some drunk asshole stumbled into me. The rim of the glass smacked me in my teeth and the beer poured onto my jacket.

Next thing I knew, Nicky had me in a bear hug. The drunk was laid out, donating a generous amount of blood to Axel's barroom floor. He made a feeble attempt to rise up on his elbows and knees. Kicked him full in the ribs as Nick tried forcing me to the door.

"Holy shit!" he said, struggling to get me into his car. "Are you like seriously deranged?"

Couldn't answer, the adrenaline burning inside.

"That guy was six six and you dropped him with one punch."

For the first time in my miserable life I was raging.

"Fuck on a bike, bro. Even I would be afraid to take your ass on. That bitch made a man of you. You're one dangerous motherfucker all of a sudden."

Dangerous, yeah, that was me. He only knew the half of it.

"Let's go," was all I said.

* * *

RIGGIO'S CLAM HOUSE was a hole in the wall, but a legendary one. Situated at the corner of Emmons Avenue and Ocean Avenue, directly across from the footbridge that spanned the ass-end of Sheepshead Bay, Riggio's had been the setting for countless shady deals and more than one mob hit. In the summer sometimes, Nicky and me used to take the bus down here and fish off the bridge. Seemed like a million fucking years ago. But so did every good thing in my life. Exercised the good sense not to try and recall what those were.

Although I had asked for the meet, it was Boyle picked the location. The prick had nothing if not a sense of drama. With him it was hard to know the reasoning behind his decisions. Him and his donkey-fucking logic. Did he just want to stick it to the guineas by talking shop on their turf? Did he already know I was a cop? Would Griffin be waiting to put one in my ear? The setting was convenient enough. Could dump my dead ass directly in Sheepshead Bay or haul it to the marshlands of nearby Gerritsen Beach. Maybe he had a boat waiting and would drop my weighted body in the Atlantic off Manhattan or Plumb Beach. There was no shortage of places to dump a body in this part of Brooklyn. Or maybe Boyle just liked raw clams.

When we got there, Nicky parked around back. The stink of the discarded seafood rotting in the dumpsters overwhelmed the smell of the sea itself. Thought, no, that rotting smell was me. If Griffin was waiting around the turn, who gave a fuck?

"What are you smiling at?" Nick wanted to know as we turned the corner.

"Nothing, Nicky. Nothing."

Boyle and Griffin were seated at a table in the rear of the dimly lit clam house. It was what you'd expect, red and white checked tablecloths, flickering candles, and Chianti bottles covered in wicker and dripped wax. Boyle got up to greet me as if I was a brother gone for five years instead of a flunky gone a month or two. Hugged me, slapped my back, tousled my hair. Griffin curled up the corner of his mouth. Said nothing. That was like effusive for him.

"Sit!" Boyle ordered. We did. "I heard of your troubles, boyo. Nothing will gut a man like a woman. You learn your lesson and move on. In the future, you won't let it happen to you again. If the opportunity should ever arise for me to teach you boys how it's done, how to deal with a woman proper, I will. That's me word. Do you think she was stepping out on you?"

"No."

"Were you on her?" he asked.

Could feel the rage again. Tasted it. *Fuck, rage had flavor and it was nothing like bacon or pussy.* How could this prick even ask me that?

"Never," I heard myself say, the rage subsiding, slightly.

Boyle must've seen it in my eyes. Seemed well pleased. "Let's order."

Boyle ordered about two dozen clams of various sorts, so I guess that cleared up any questions I had about why we were here.

During dinner, Nick described what I'd done to the big man at Axel's. Now it was Griffin who seemed impressed. Actually stopped chewing for a second.

"Listen, Todd," Boyle said between bites of cheese cake, "I've a partner in South Boston could use an extra hand for a coupl'a weeks, someone from outside his patch, if you catch my drift. Would you be interested in doing me the favor? Seems to me you could use the distraction and I would be inclined to show my appreciation."

"Would I get to use my hands?"

"Idle hands are the devil's playground, so it's said. Well, the devil don't do much playing in South Boston."

Later learned, and at quite a cost, his assessment was as wrong as wrong could be.

"When do I leave?"

"Not before dessert, at least. Eat up."

"He was one of those guys, that rare breed, that when people mentioned his name they'd automatically lower their voices and mentally make the sign of the cross."

—Rick Marinick, *Boyos*

A WEEK AT home hadn't done much but make things worse. My nerves were raw, ends frayed by the time I hit the Boston train. Think I would have walked if Boyle had asked. Wanted out, out of my dad's house, out of Brooklyn, out of my own skin. Settled for out of Brooklyn.

I'd seen Boyle only once again after our dinner in Sheepshead Bay, back at his office, Griffin, as always, by his side. It was then he handed me my ticket and an envelope fat with cash.

"You mind yourself," he said. "Rudi's a tough son of a bitch, but do what he says and you'll be well served."

"What's the money for?"

"Think of it as an advance."

"An advance?"

"Don't worry, boyo. You'll earn every penny."

Griffin curled his lip at that. Nodded his head slightly in agreement. This was serious. For Griffin this was practically a display of fear. I didn't give a shit. Thought, bring it on. Bring the fucker on. Went back to Brooklyn, laid in my bedroom for days trying not to think about what I couldn't stop thinking about. Memory is the curse of humankind. Wondered did dogs or cats torture themselves this way? Christ, hoped not, the poor fuckers. Nicky kept calling. Went drinking with him again, but only for an hour and not at Axel's. Tried to bring Leeza up once. Saw the look on my puss and segued quickly to another subject. Smart man, my old pal Nick. My dad steered clear. The only time in my life I appreciated his near invisibility. *Thanks, pops!*

Dreamed a lot during the week. Kept picturing Leeza swinging from the big old oak in front of our house. Could never see her face in the dreams, but I knew it was her. The neighbors didn't seem to notice or, if they did, they didn't care. Apparently, as long as it wasn't that miserable bitch Sophie, any naked woman could hang herself in front of my old house. Wonder what Robert Frost would have made of my neighbors. And yeah, fuckhead, I know who Robert Frost was.

The whole train ride up I occupied myself by thinking of just how O'Connor knew I'd be asked up to Boston. Was he like psychic? Maybe he'd called the Psychic Hotline and they'd seen it in the stars. *You'll meet the woman of your dreams. You'll have a bright future if you invest in high tech start-ups. And, by the way, that schmuck you're training will be asked to work in Boston.* Somehow doubted that's the way it went.

O'Connor had a snitch on the inside in Boston. That gave me cold comfort. Meant that someone up there would know who I was, what I was. Didn't need police training to know that a rat has a peculiar sense of loyalty, loyalty to self. If the rat was willing to flip on a guy who scared Griffin, he wouldn't think twice about rolling on me to save his own neck. Brooklyn schooled me on that.

Boston, Philadelphia, anywhere: all equals to me. A fat, unshaven bastard with a wind-fucked comb-over met me at the station. Smelled like beer and onions and his jeans rode low enough to reveal the top of his plumber's crack. Delightful. Said his name was Finney. Guess I believed him. Didn't offer to shake my hand. Worked for me. Wanted as little personal contact with old Finney as could be managed. Just sitting in the front seat of his 1979 Buick Electra 225 made me want to shower. The vinyl stank worse than the driver and the carpeting, what was left of it, was covered in cigarette filters, beer cans, and porno magazines.

"Watch the hole in the floor," was the other sentence Finney had uttered.

Oh, didn't I mention the fucking floor had rusted through and I could see the streets of Boston close up as we went to wherever it was we were going? Well, I thought, it was only up from here. Shows you what I knew.

Rode into a dingy area of crooked streets, wood row houses, and bleak faces. Was like the sun didn't shine on this part of town. Reminded me of the pictures from my history textbooks of nineteenth century England. The kids on the streets moved like snakes, wary and coiled to strike. Knew the posture well. Thought Nicky might have liked it here, Nicky or the Artful Dodger. Finney stopped in an alleyway behind a small brick warehouse.

The fat man pointed at the backdoor like the ghost of Christmas Future pointing at my grave. He was his usual talkative self. Wondered who'd win the debate between him and Griffin. Griffin, no doubt. He'd just cut Finney's fat throat. Stepped through the door into New England's contribution to my personal hell.

Inside was musty, dank, but an improvement indeed over close proximity to Finney. There was no one around. A step van that had been crudely painted brown with rollers and brushes was backed up to a quiet loading dock. Then above me, at my back, I heard a muffled knocking. Turned to see a man at the window of a second floor office gesturing me to come up. Found the stairs.

Satan was a skinny fucker with wispy gray hair, keen blue eyes and a happy mouth too big for his gaunt face.

"Take a load off, fella." He smiled broad and bright as the gates to heaven. An unlit cigarette dangled from his lower lip as he spoke. Must've been glued on as it never once seemed in danger of falling. "Jaysus, ya must be wrecked from yer trip. Sorry ya had to suffer Finney's company, but I had no one else available to send for ya. A beer." It wasn't really a question.

"Sure."

He handed me a Sam Adams, cold as Griffin's heart. Sat myself down in an ancient office chair.

"Love the stuff me own self," he said, taking a bottle. "That Harp shite from home is but blond piss for pussies." And like Griffin, this guy was a native speaker, not the cartoon equivalent. "I'm Rudi. It's not me given name, but it's who I am. And you'd be Todd?"

"I would."

"I know you boys down there in Brooklyn are tough fookers, but this is a different world. The rules of the road don't apply."

"Figure that's why I'm here."

"Boyle told me ya were a smart bastard. I like that. The less I need explain, the greater the benefit. Better to say nowt to a man who can read a map for himself."

Just shook my head and drank.

He smiled that smile at me again. The sun might not shine outside, but it did in here. Rudi seemed as fierce as a twig and with as much heft. Guessed he liked it that way. Always better to be underestimated. He could see me sizing him up. Read my mind.

"Prefer to be underestimated, I do, and never to make the same mistake about my enemies. You'd figured by now that I'm not sweet as cane sugar and you'd be right. Did Griffin not say anything about me to ya?"

"Griffin doesn't say anything to anyone about anybody, but his face speaks sometimes. That was enough for me."

"Good. Let's be off. I'll drop you at your place in Cambridge."

"Cambridge?"

"Yer no Southie," he said, showing me out to his '85 Coupe de Ville. "Besides, you've already served half yer purpose in me having ya up here."

"Finney," I said.

"Jaysus and his blessed mother, yer even smarter than advertised. Before we get halfway to yer flat, he will have told me boyos about ya."

"They'll figure I'm outside talent brought in to see to one of them. You wanna see who runs and who stays. You've got a rat problem."

"Feckin' rodents. Easy to kill 'em, but tough to flush the fookers out a their holes. If ya were ever to tire of working for Boyle, I'd take ya on."

Ignored that. "Funny thing about Finney, you say he's a talker, but he said no more than ten words to me from the time he picked me up at the station."

"He wouldn't talk to ya, now would he?"

"You think he's the snitch?"

Rudi had a good laugh at that. His laugh, like the rest of him, could fool you. It was deep and resonant. "Not Finney. He's a stupid bastard. Good for collections and the occasional muscle, but would have neither the stones nor the wherewithal to parlay what little he knows into transit fare. No, it's one of the smart ones. Always is," he said, staring right at me.

"Hey, don't look at me! I just got here."

He laughed again. Good thing one of us did.

My flat was a one bedroom rented apartment on the top floor of a small Victorian just off Massachusetts Avenue. It was as close to Harvard as I was likely to get. My destiny, always a few blocks from the Ivy League. Handed me an envelope not nearly as fat as the one Boyle had given me.

"The key's in there along with a small wedge. I own the building under another name, so no one will bother ya here. It should be a while till I call again, so relax a bit. Learn the city's charms, which are legion. Catch a ball game at Fenway. Locally, there's a fine barbeque establishment just down the block and bookstore around the bend there on Mass Ave."

"Thanks, Rudi." Shook his hand.

"If things work as I hope, please God, it's me that'll be thanking you. By the way, feel free to use the phone and the appliances. Enjoy yer time in Boston."

Watched him drive away, the taillights of his old Cadillac disappearing around the corner. Between Finney and Rudi their rides were older than time itself. At least Rudi's Caddy had solid floorboards. And they call Jews cheap. No, it was real estate above all else made an Irishman feel wealthy. The rest of the trappings were inconsequential. Boyle too had most of his holdings in real estate. Guess maybe they had a point.

The apartment had its own entrance in the rear and was spotlessly clean and stocked with furniture older than manned space flight. But it was good solid furniture, if not exactly trend-setting in style. The appliances, however, were bizarrely incongruous. There was like a huge flat screen TV in the living room. There was a restaurant quality Viking stove and a Sub Zero fridge in the kitchen. Assumed all the appliances had fallen off the truck at Logan Airport or on the piers. It was just the same at JFK. If it fell off the truck on Monday, I was wearing it, using it, or selling it by Wednesday.

Unpacked my suitcase and checked out the fridge. It was empty but for a six pack of Sam Adams. Took one and plopped myself down on the plaid cushions of the colonial couch and learned the ins and outs of my big screen TV. Strange, but an hour had passed without me once thinking of Philly or Leeza or O'Connor. Thought I might get to like Boston. Even fell into the first dreamless, peaceful sleep I'd had in some time.

Waking, I felt as if I could breathe again. Leeza was there, front and center, but some of the bitter edge had been bevelled off. The windows had darkened and, for a change, the hunger was in my belly instead of my heart.

After a half rack of ribs, pulled pork and a beer at the barbeque joint Rudi had recommended, walked past my new house on the way to the bookstore he'd mentioned.

It wasn't like any kind of bookstore I'd ever been in before. It was on the ground floor of a red clapboard house and the only stuff they stocked were mysteries and detective novels. Never been much for fiction, let alone crime novels. I mean, like I didn't have to make it up, right? The occasional book next to my bed would be about WWII or the building of the atomic bomb or some such shit.

Felt more lost in that bookstore than I did in Philly. It was like wall to wall books with huge stacks piled up in the aisles. The paperbacks were squeezed so tightly together you wouldn't've been able to fit a dancing angel between any two of them.

"You seem like you can use some help," an invisible voice called to me.

Looked around and there, seated behind the counter, was a big earth momma with a friendly face. She wore glasses, let her hair straggle, but had a presence that was hard to explain.

"Not much for fiction," I said.

"Don't read this stuff, huh?"

"Never."

She called out to someone lurking in the stacks. "*Continental Op. Maltese Falcon. Red Harvest. The Long Goodbye. Farewell, My Lovely. The Little Sister.*" Then she turned back to me. "Visiting?"

"Moved in around the corner."

A spinster-ish woman appeared before us with six paperbacks in her hands. She placed them on the counter and receded into the shadows.

"Here," the earth momma said, putting the books in a bag. "You take those and see what you think."

Reached for my wallet, but she waved me off. "You'll be back. Pay me then."

"Seem pretty sure about that."

"I been in the business a long time. I'll take my chances on you."

Didn't argue. Thanked her and dropped the bag at the apartment. Stared at the phone and thought about calling Nick. Didn't. What would I have said? That I had bought books? Might have impressed Nick's dad, but not Nicky. Wasn't sure what would impress him anymore. Felt the walls closing in. Like I said, the edge was off a bit, not gone.

Found a bar near Harvard Square, an Irish pub. Big surprise, right? Like finding salt in the ocean. It was pretty empty. Ordered a Harpoon Ale, turned to watch the Red Sox game on the tube. Didn't actually give a fuck about the Red Sox. No Yankee fan could say that. Sometimes, it seemed Yankee fans like Nick cared more about the Red Sox failing than the Yankees winning. Failing, now there's something I was well acquainted with, being raised a Mets fan and all.

When I turned away from the game, noticed a cute blonde in jeans and a Red Sox sweatshirt had seated herself two stools away from me. She ordered a Jack Daniel's with no back and began chatting with the barman. He didn't seem terribly interested. Under normal circumstances I would have shared his lack of enthusiasm. Short, perky blondes with cropped hair, a little thick through the hips, aren't usually my type, but she had such fiery blue eyes that I found myself staring at her. Suppose I wasn't doing a very good job of disguising my curiosity.

"Fah chrissakes, mista, ya stare any hadah at me and ya'll see into my childhood."

"Sorry."

"Don't apologize, just buy a girl a drink."

Told the bartender to put her drinks on my tab. Between Rudi and Boyle's scratch, I was well set for cash. She moved over to sit beside me. We clinked glasses.

"New Yawka, huh?" she said.

"Brooklynite."

"Yankees?"

"Mets."

"Both bad answers in this town, but ya got some stones on ya fer saying. Here's to ya."

"To the Sox," I said.

We both emptied our glasses. Gave the sign to the bartender for another round.

"Kathleen Dolan."

"Todd Rosen."

We shook and finished the second round at a reasonable pace. Explained that she worked at Harvard as a square badge. It bored the shit out of her, but it paid the rent. I ad-libbed some crap about being a consultant to a computer company and that I had a couple of weeks in town before I started.

"Evah been to Fenway?"

"Nope."

"Friday night. They're playing Detroit. I got two tickets, wanna come?"

"Sure."

"Meet me here at five-thirty."

"Deal."

We shook on it.

Three beers later, headed back to my new place. Kathleen was finishing her last Jack when I left. She'd probably have come home with me if I asked. Didn't. The more I drank, the more present Leeza became. If I ever bedded Kathleen, didn't want Leeza looking over my shoulder. That night in bed it was just me and Raymond Chandler.

* * *

KATHLEEN AND I went to the Sox game that Friday night and sat next to the foul pole in the right field corner. Baseball in Fenway was a much more intimate experience than at Shea or Yankee Stadium. There was a charm to it. Charm is not a New York thing. The grand scale of everything in New York suffocates charm in the crib. The Sox won like fifteen to twelve, a real fucking pitchers' duel.

Kathleen had a beer an inning until the fifth and slowed to one every other inning for the rest of the game. Good thing there were no extra innings. When the game was over, I suggested we find a local bar. She suggested we go fuck. Liked her suggestion better.

We went back to her place, a first floor apartment in a non-descript neighborhood.

Kathleen's definition of foreplay was another two beers. When she was done with the second, she just pulled her clothes off and sort of shoved me into the bedroom. Fucked for hours. She had to be raw about halfway through, but I don't think she cared. It was her nature to just carry on. It wasn't the greatest sex, certainly not the most tender, but it was completely without pretense or baggage. When she wanted something, wanted to be touched in a particular spot in a particular way, Kathleen just told me. I did the same. The sex, as it rarely ever is, was about the sex.

There was no cooing or hand holding come the morning, no whispers or soft kisses on the ear. We had fun. We fucked. Now one of us had to go to work. When I opened my eyes, Kathleen was wearing her rent-a-cop get up.

"The hot watah's not great," she said. "Can ya get back to yer place from here?"

"I'll find my way. Thanks for the game."

"Thanks fah the beers and the ride."

"Anytime."

"Next week sometime?"

"Sure."

And that was it. Kathleen became part of my routine, my rebound fuck buddy. Twice a week, we'd get together, get drunk and just fuck our brains out. Knew less about her than I knew about Leeza. Ninety-five percent of what Kathleen knew about me was a lie. Perfection.

Varied from our usual gig only once. Took her niece Bonnie to the zoo. Cute as a button, precocious as hell, but it was Kathleen who was the real kid. Between our beer, baseball, and balling, Kathleen and I didn't get around to our childhoods much. Knew why I avoided the subject. Didn't have to be a fucking genius to see that her childhood had been rough. My guess, she'd never been to a zoo before. Caught a contact buzz from being around her she was so juiced by it. Two hours in, Bonnie was asleep on my shoulder. Kathleen just had to experience the whole place.

Made me see Kathleen in a different light. Was she Leeza? No. No one would fill that space, ever. But a man could do worse than settling into a comfortable life with her. I was apt to do much worse. That night, the sex got as close to tender as it was ever going to get between us.

Rest of my routine was less exciting, but no less fun. Was at the bookstore every other day buying whatever the earth momma suggested. It got so that I barely watched the ginormous TV in the apartment. Ate at the barbeque place almost every night. Realized this was the first time since I was a kid that my life had settled into a pleasant rhythm. As a kid, there was school, ball, and TV. Every day when I woke up, I knew what was ahead.

But unlike when I was a kid, I knew this pleasant rhythm would come crashing down around my head. Can't lie to you. The clock was ticking. Heard it louder by the day. Understood that this wasn't some paid vacation, that Rudi would come calling, that Leeza wouldn't, that Nicky, Boyle, and Griffin were still back home. Worst was waiting for O'Connor. The tick-tocking was loudest for him. It was near closing time and I was in the back room of the bookstore when the clock stopped.

"Find what you're looking for, lad?"

O'Connor.

"Didn't expect to find you. Not here, anyway."

"And why not here?" He seemed hurt.

"What's going on?"

"There's been a spot of trouble, son. Time to close shop and get you home."

"But—"

"But nothing. We're pulling you. Don't worry, you'll get your shield."

"Don't give a shit about my shield. What the fuck happened?"

"Seems the Boston PD sprung a leak and you might have been compromised."

"Does Rudi know? Boyle?"

"We don't think so, at least not yet. We wouldn't be having this conversation if they did. That's why we're moving you out. Go get your stuff. Here's a ticket for the air shuttle out of Logan for tomorrow morning. There's a reservation for a Bob Smith at the Holiday Inn. Stay there tonight. And don't worry, we've got your back. There's two men on you. Sorry, lad."

He left. I was frozen in place. Didn't want to go. Liked my life as it was, artificial as it might be. On my way out, leaned over and kissed the earth momma goodbye.

"No books today. Didn't find what you wanted?"

"Yes and no," I said. "Yes and no."

Not that I ever got mail, but still always checked as I made my way up to my apartment. This evening there was an envelope. No stamp, no return address, just a bloody thumb print. Inside the envelope was Kathleen's square badge and a scrap of paper with an address on it. Suppose the smart thing would have been to throw it in the trash, get to the Holiday Inn, and try hard to forget Boston. Like I said, I wasn't as smart as my mom.

Spotted the two cops in an unmarked unit across the street from my apartment. Went out the back, climbed the fence, called a cab. Gave a false destination to the dispatcher. When the hack showed, shoved a hundred dollar bill in the cabbie's hand, gave him the real address, asked him not to put this ride on the meter and not to write it down on his trip sheet. Didn't have to ask twice. Also asked him to stop at a payphone when we got close to the address.

"We're about two miles away," he said and handed me his cell phone.

Dialed the number wrong a few times, then got it right. Whispered into the mouth piece. Erased the call off his phone and handed it back.

"How close are we now?" I asked.

"Two blocks."

"Stop and point the way."

He was happy to oblige, especially after I put another hundred in his hand. As he turned back around, pressed the cold muzzle of my .38 to the nape of his neck.

"If you fuck with me and I find out you took my money and opened your mouth, I'll hunt you down and shoot you through the liver. Do we understand one another?"

He nodded that he did. When I got out, he didn't wait to see if I was moving in the right direction. Soon the only trace of the cab having ever been there was the faint smell of its exhaust.

Street was a fucking wreck. Every other house had a foreclosure sign up on its dirt and hardscrabble lawn. And it wasn't like the rest of the homes were candidates for a glossy photo shoot. The second most popular sign on the block was BEWARE OF DOG. Would have to be aware of more than just pit bulls and Rottweilers. There were tire-less cars up on cinder blocks behind the cyclone fencing in nearly every yard. The one good thing about the ruined landscape was that I could very clearly see the house that belonged to the address written on the scrap of paper in my pocket. It was the only well-lit place on the block.

Finney's rusted piece of shit was parked out front. A guy whose face I could not make out, but who was way too thin to be Finney, was pacing a rut in the broken sidewalk. The red glowing tip of his cigarette zigzagged back and forth, back and forth. My bet was there was at least one other guy around beside the one out front and Finney. Not like I was a novice at this crap. When I did "jobs" for Boyle, he didn't send his whole crew. Usually two or three guys, four at most. The more people you involve, the greater the chances are that someone will fuck up. The more people involved, the harder it is to keep control. Conversely, the fewer people in on a job, the fewer that can get caught or flip.

Had to move fast. Got down in a crouch, moving quickly and quietly along the same side of the street as the house in which I assumed Kathleen was being held. Passing each house, I'd silently swing open their front gates. Then I'd pull the gate close to me so that I was sandwiched between the gate and the fence at my back. First and second houses yielded nothing. House number three? Bingo! A humongous Rottweiler came barreling through the open gate. Made an attempt to get at me, but after snagging a tooth on the fencing, he gave up, moving on to the next best target; the shithead pacing in front of the target house. Let the massive fucker get a good twenty feet ahead of me before following. Didn't want him to change his mind or direction.

The relative silence of the night was broken by a sickening scream. The dog was all over the cigarette smoker. The Rottweiler growled as he tore into the man's flesh. Got close enough to see the blood come shooting out of the guy's thigh. The thin bastard was smart enough to try and guard his throat from the dog, but made the mistake of going for his piece. As soon as he removed one hand from his throat, the Rottweiler went for it. Now the man was flailing aimlessly, panic having overwhelmed him.

Another man, big, built like a middle linebacker, came charging out of the house, a 9mm or .40 caliber in his hand. He tried pulling the dog off his friend with his free hand, but when he saw that wasn't going to work, he blew a hole through the Rottweiler's massive head. The dog collapsed and the shooter pushed him off his partner. The thin guy's body was twitching, blood pouring out of his neck with decreasing force. When the big guy knelt down to see if he could help, I whacked him across the back of his skull with a chunk of concrete. He went down but not immediately out. Took care of that with a kick to his jaw. Heard his neck snap. Added both dead men's guns to my collection.

Thought about throwing something through the front window and sneaking around back. Didn't have the time. Charged through the front door, a pistol in each hand. Nothing. Then the house went dark. Blackness. Heavy steps. Floorboards creaking. Heard a sound that would make even the bravest man shiver. *Cha-ching!* A shotgun being racked. Something hard and round pressed into my ribs.

"Move asshole!" Finney.

Got me to the basement door and shoved me down the steps. Didn't lose consciousness when I hit the wet floor, but I was a little disoriented. Listened to his heavy steps behind me. Smelled him as he stepped over me. Beer, sex, and onions. His meaty paws yanking out the guns still clutched in my hands. He tossed them. Stepped away. A switch clicked. Lights came on. Wish they hadn't.

The basement floor was wet not with water but with blood. A foot or two away from me was a very naked, very dead man. Even in my hazy state of awareness, I could tell he was worse for wear. There was a hunting knife sticking out from where his left eye used to sit. There were burn marks and welts all over his body. And as my eyes refocused, I noticed his ears had been crudely sliced off. The thickened blood on the sides of his head told me that he'd been alive when the ears were removed. Another part of his anatomy had also been removed and relocated to his mouth. Was glad to have missed the butchering.

Heard something, a muffled moan. *Kathleen!*

"Get up, pig!" Finney ordered, shotgun pointed at my chest.

Kathleen was nude, tied down to a workbench with wire that had cut through her wrists and ankles. Her head was clamped in a vise. Duct tape covered her mouth. She too had cigarette burns on her body.

Charged. "You motherfucker! I'll—"

He swung the butt of the shotgun and caught me in the jaw. I staggered backwards nearly tripping over the dead man, but didn't go down. My back was now against the wall of the basement.

"Shut the fuck up!" he barked. "You piece a shit cop. See that rat on the floor there? That snitch fuck was Rudi's favorite boyo. Good thing I know people on the cops who like to earn on the side or that cocksucker woulda brought us all down. Take a good fucking look at him. That's where you're headed in a few minutes. But first I'm gonna make you watch me kill your girlfriend here."

"Leave her the fuck alone!"

"Shut your fucking mouth!" He waved the shotgun at me again. "Besides, she's already asked me to kill her about twenty times already. The first time I stuck my cock in her asshole, she practically fucking begged me. She didn't like it too much either when I squeezed her head a little. Like this."

He stepped by the bench, took a hand off the scatter gun, ripped the tape off her mouth, and twisted the vise handle. Kathleen's squealed. Her body jerked with pain, the wire biting further into her flesh. A car pulled to the curb outside. Finney heard the car too. He looked up. Had to move now.

Reached behind me and retrieved the .38 tucked between my belt and the small of my back. The stupid fat fuck had neglected to roll me over when he took the guns out of my hands. First shot caught him slightly above the heart. He twisted to his right. The shotgun flashed, then roared. Second shot caught him in the side of the head. He was on his way to hell before he hit the floor. Heard voices upstairs, feet rushing, pounding. Finney had fulfilled Kathleen's wish. He'd killed her. The shotgun blast had torn away the left side of her chest. By the time they pulled me off Finney's lifeless carcass, I had nearly cut his head off using the hunting knife. And by that time, I had come to realize I'd done as much as Finney to seal Kathleen's fate. Griffin's words about violence rang in my ears. *Once you cross the line, you cross the line.*

"Ah, jaysus!" Rudi.

Turned to see him crossing himself. That was the last bit of humanity in him.

"Start talking, boyo." He eyed me coldly, pressing the still smoking shotgun to my temple. I'd seen more compassion in the eyes of an insect.

"Well, I served my purpose. There's your rat," I said, pointing at Finney. "This dead guy here missing his ears and the eye was like that when I got here. Finney didn't mention his name."

"Tommy Mac," Rudi obliged.

"Tommy Mac found out about Finney from a source inside the cops. At least that's what Finney said. So Finney killed him and then lured me down here by. . . Well, you can see how. He was going to set it up that Tommy Mac was the rat, that I found out about it. Finney was gonna make it look like Tommy Mac killed me and the girl. Finney was gonna come to the rescue, but too late. Then he would prove his loyalty to you by torturing the rat to death. His ass would be covered and he'd be even closer to you."

Story had holes, but it was pretty good given that I'd just killed my first three men and was half crazy with guilt. Rudi wasn't buying it.

"Might believe it if it were any man but Finney."

"You said it your own self, Rudi. You underestimated him."

Nothing convinces a man better than his own words thrown back in his face. I saw Rudi's eyes return to their mammalian incarnation and knew I had saved my fairly worthless life. He pulled the shotgun away.

"Ya done good, pal. There'll be a bonus in it for ya."

Not an "I'm sorry about the girl" or "What a terrible price to have to pay", but a bonus.

"Take him back to the safehouse and get him fixed up," Rudi said to one of his minions.

Felt hands lifting me up and moving me along.

"What about—?"

"Quiet now, boyo," he shushed me. "I'll clean up the mess.

In that second, I came to hate Rudi more than I could ever hate Finney or anyone else. Ever!

"What did their purpose conceal
If not the simplest units of friendship?
Like a ship returning in a foreign language
They have turned into beasts, conscious only
Of one another, blind to perfection,
Finding peace only in each other's arms."
    —John Koethe, from his poem "The Friendly Animals"

NEVER BELIEVED IN absolutes before Kathleen's murder. Did now, absolutely. Was FFL. Fucked for life, that was me. There was no escaping culpability. Her blood was on me sure as my own skin. But her death led to a kind of clarity about the universe that had until then eluded me. When my mother took her own life, it was as much relief as loss. Only my dad cried. Then, for himself, really. This was different. Death and me, we were no longer going to stare at each other from across the dance floor. Once you feel loss, you always feel it.

O'Connor was neither fool nor saint. Let me be for a time. Drifted back into my life in New York like carbon monoxide: deadly and colorless. Boyle, Nicky, and Griffin folded me back under their wings without a second thought. In fact, I was treated with a newfound respect. Obviously, Rudi had let word leak back home about my making my bones, about the scene in the basement. Found myself wondering sometimes if Rudi hadn't had his boyos take pictures of the carnage. Had an image of him staring at photos of Kathleen's decimated body and masturbating. Christ, those were the nights I drank myself to sleep. As angry as I was at him, it wasn't Rudi who killed her.

My two-week grace period was over and O'Connor had me meet him at the Einstein gravesite. Never would have visited my mom's grave if it wasn't for O'Connor. Was like a fringe benefit.

"That was some ugly shit in Boston, lad. You comported yourself well," he said.

"Comported! Is that one in the glossary of the cop handbook?"

"We've business to do, so—"

"Do you know what they did with her body?" Couldn't let Kathleen be brushed off like that.

"It won't do you any good to—"

"Do you know if they even buried her?"

No idiot, he saw that he was going to have to answer if we were to move on. "They probably didn't bury her, no."

"What then?"

For the first time I could see in him a split between the human being and the cop. The human being didn't want to tell me. The cop understood that the truth would fuel me. The cop won out. "They might've hacked her up and scattered her in dumps or fed her to—"

For the second time I vomited on poor Sonya Einstein's grave. "I want to get these motherfuckers, all of them!"

"Okay then, let's get to work."

When he left, I did actually go stand by my mother's grave. "So," I said, "this is what real pain feels like. I still can't forgive you, but maybe I understand a little better."

Was the first and last time in my life I talked to a patch of dirt and blades of grass.

* * *

BROOKLYN.
  Axel's.

The place was no longer a touchstone for my obsession with Leeza Velez. Given my time in Boston, Leeza's memory was more like a faint ringing in the ears. After what had happened, I couldn't even think of Leeza and me together. Felt dirty, a leper, that to imagine us together was sin. Not a God sin. Gotten over that bullshit concept fresh out of the womb. Was worried I'd rub off on her, stain her somehow. What the fuck was I worried about, anyway? I was never going to see her again. Leeza Velez, gone to me as my mother.

Nicky was sitting next to me. Whatever had happened between us in the past year didn't seem to matter much to either of us. Good definition of friendship that. Took comfort in his presence and he in mine. In my eyes, he was like immune to my disease. He was the only friend I had, the only friend I was ever going to have. The cop shit? That was something else. Would have to work that out later. He was okay with the silence between us, but broke it with whispered curiosity.

"The fuck happened down there?"

Ah fuck! The question hit me between the shoulder blades. Sucked down my Jack on the rocks and chased it with cold Sam Adams. Had taken to drinking Jack to honor Kathleen. Crap! Fuck that lie. Had taken to drinking it to torture and anesthetize myself. The Jack burned, felt my face flush. Said,

"Shit happened."

We left it at that.

* * *

A WEEK LATER, I put in motion the wheels of destruction.

Nick and I were casing an apartment, at least that's what he thought we were doing. We were getting high, Yankee game on the radio in the background. Noticed he couldn't keep his mind on the job for listening to the game. Busted his balls, told him I'd become a true Red Sox fan. Nearly shit his pants.

"The freaking Sox! You're a Yankees' fan, the fuck you think you can switch like that, it's as bad as that asswipe who sold the Dodgers."

"O'Malley," I corrected, "didn't sell the Dodgers. He moved 'em."

"That shanty prick." Nick was riled. "Fuck 'im!"

"Nick, not for nothing, but I've been a Mets fan all my life."

"I don't think I ever knew that." Oblivious. Typical Yankee fan. "Still a betrayal."

Guess he was right. Laughed. "Nicky, everything changes."

"Fuck you!" Didn't like my answer.

In a talkative mood that night, Nick was. Asked me what the deal was with South Philly then South Boston. Nearly bit through my tongue against the notion of confessing my new allegiance and describing, in exquisite detail what a woman's body looks like after it's been cut with wires, burned with cigarettes, and been hit at close range with buckshot. Forced myself to focus squarely on the building we were casing.

"Buddy," I said, "one way or another, the business we're in, everything goes south."

He tried patting me on the shoulder. Seemed he was feeling sorry for himself. Wasn't in the mood for it, not after thinking about Kathleen. Told him not to make a habit of giving me reassuring pats. The doorman did as he'd been told and abandoned his spot in the lobby. The wheels turned. Time to move.

At the door of the apartment I made like Houdini and picked the lock. Movies and TV really fuck with a man's head. Even semi-hard guys like Nicky could be fooled. They see a guy pick a lock in ten seconds on the tube and they're like convinced it's a breeze. Isn't. Try it some time, see how far you get. All I did was stick one thin pick in top of the keyhole, a crooked one in the bottom and jiggle. *Voila!* Here's a tip. Really helps when the lock is already open. Nicky was impressed. That's all that mattered.

He was further impressed by the size and décor of the apartment. Me too. There were original artworks up on the walls and pieces of furniture that cost more than my dad's house. Never understood how something or some place could smell like money. Did now. Reeked of it. Wondered if it clung to you like cigarette smoke.

"Remember. Cash, dope, and jewelry."

Nick couldn't believe it. "We're leaving this? This shit must be worth a bundle."

Told him art was a pain in the balls to fence. He started going for a painting, anyway. Shook my head and went into the bedroom. That's when the fireworks began.

Door opened.

Stockbroker type. Brooks Brothers suit. "What the fuck is this?"

I walked out of the bedroom. "Fuck."

Shot the guy in the mouth, twice for good measure. Ruined his suit. His head wasn't looking all that well either.

"This piece of shit keeps jumping," I said, looking down at the cheap knock off of a .357 Magnum. "I was going for the heart. Next time, I bring a Glock."

The look on Nick's face was priceless. *Next time*! Made him help me drag the stiff into the bathroom. Amazing what squibs and a little makeup can do. Nick was so fucked, he grabbed a bottle of Makers Mark and took a mighty gulp. Warned him not to drink while we were on the job. Asked if I was going to shoot him to.

Looked at him stone cold. "If I have to."

He wiped the bottle down and put it back.

We collected our take in a black plastic garbage bag and split. On the way out, he wanted to know if killing the guy was really necessary.

"Probably," I said.

On the ride to Boyle's, I kept it up, the cold-blooded killer routine. Seemed to really get to Nicky. Good. Getting him the fuck out of this life wouldn't be such a bad thing. Kept shaking his head. Couldn't believe I'd just killed a man and could be so cool about it. I lit up a cigarette. New habit. Might kill me, but what the fuck. Reaching for my pack in the glove box, I saw fear in Nicky's eyes. Rare sight that. Did he think I was going for a gun? He seemed to want to rehash things. He was still a bit in shock.

"It's over," I said, and not friendly-like. "You wanna dwell on it, replay it, do it on your own nickel."

That just pissed him off and he started cracking his fucking knuckles. Made me mental. Wanted to know what had happened to me since Boston. Said he didn't know me anymore. That made two of us. When we pulled up in front of Boyle's warehouse, warned Nicky not to tell the boss about the mess back at the apartment, that there was no need to get into it now. Thought Nicky would shit.

Biblical Boyle was an ambitious prick who had worked his way up the sewer pipe to the toilet and from the toilet to the gutter. All the time he was climbing he carried the good book by his side, the stupid dick. Samuel L. Jackson had worn that biblical shit out two movies ago. But like I said before, Boyle's ambition would carry him only as far as Griffin's psychopathy. Love that word, psychopathy. As we entered, I warned Nick to keep his eyes on Griffin.

"Why?" Nick asked.

Sighed like a disappointed parent. "Because *he'll* be watching you."

It was odd. My whole miserable life, I looked to Nicky to be the teacher. Now the world had flipped. Philly, Boston, they'd made me the teacher and there was another lesson coming up.

Boyle acted well pleased with the take from our job. Offered us a seat and a drink of Jameson. Three shot glasses. Only two were raised. Wasn't in the mood to drink with the likes of him or Rudi. Also wanted to make a point to the man: I don't fear you. Maybe I did, but I was too numb just then to realize it.

When I refused his hospitality, his eyes went all fish-like and cold. Swept my untouched glass of Irish off the desk, the whiskey just missing me. Never moved. Don't even think I blinked. He and Nicky gulped their shots down.

"Back home, you refuse to drink with a man, might be seen as an insult."

Christ, what a straight line. *Back home! Where? The Bronx!* Bit my lower lip, looked at the shot glass near my boot.

"We're a long way from Tipperary, Mr. Boyle."

He didn't bite. "Aye, you're right there, boyo."

Griffin smiled. Couldn't tell if he liked the joke or the size of my *cojones*. Boyle ordered me over to the piers to help smooth some goods through customs. As I headed out the door, Boyle asked if there'd been any trouble on the job tonight.

"Nothing major," I said. "Nick, your laddie . . . had to shoot the owner."

Didn't look back.

" 'You a paisan?'

'No,' I said. 'I'm a mick.'

'You're on the wrong crew. How come you ain't driving nails?'

'I'm a spy.' "

—SJ Rozan, No Colder Place

MY ZOMBIE TWIN, Nick.

Something had happened to him in the few days between the charade at the heist and this evening. Wouldn't talk about it. Couldn't very well throw stones at him given my closed mouth. Was fucking eerie though, like looking in the mirror at myself the day after Kathleen's death. Had that same haunted look. The world had shifted beneath his feet. All the assumptions that let him sleep at night had been yanked out from under him.

O'Connor had told me in no uncertain terms that I was not to push Boyle and his boyos too far.

"That was foolish, lad, not drinking with him like that. What were you out to prove?"

The prick was right, of course. As big a dick as Boyle was, he hadn't anything to do with Kathleen's murder, not really. My fight was with Rudi, the calculating, cold-hearted cocksucker, and it was a score I meant to have someday. O'Connor instructed me to find a woman to date or he'd supply me with window dressing. Fuck no. The last time he'd made that arrangement her name was Leeza Velez. Wasn't driving up that street again.

Found her at the Midori makeup counter at Bloomingdale's. Dark and darkly complected; Leeza Velez without the afterburner. Lived on Long Island and traveled all the way into Manhattan just to be able to say she worked at Bloomies in the city. What can I say, some people aim low. Who the fuck was I to judge? Liked her voice, I guess, husky and resonant. There was a point in my life not too long ago, would have killed to hear her whisper, "Fuck me. Fuck me hard." Now all I wanted to hear her say was, "Yes, come by around ten." I'd tell you her name if I could remember it. Also don't recall if it was Nicky or me that picked the place.

Took her to some joint on Lex called Rocky Sullivan's. Christ, it was like a freaking Irish theme park: St. Patty's World. No Mickey Mouse, just micks, wall to wall. The lot of them pining for the old country to which they'd never been and from which their ancestors couldn't run fast enough. There's some commonality between the Irish and the Jews, but this wasn't one of the areas of overlap. You don't hear too many second generation Jews pining for Poland or Russia, Romania or Ukraine.

That it was Mickville was bad enough, but that it was open mic night made me want to poke my eyes out. It's one thing to think you can sing. It's another to think you're funny. But, Jesus, worst of all were the ones who did the poetry. Poetry is hard enough to pull off when you've got some facility for it. When it's that over earnest, sentimental rhyming crap . . . Drove me over the edge. Talked sports with what's-her-name. Nick like couldn't believe I was with this woman and I'm talking Red Sox baseball.

Not sure where Nicky was at, truth be told. He seemed intent on seeing how much Jim Beam and Sam Adams he could ingest.

"Here's to the Yankees!" he shouted.

Other drunks joined his fool's chorus.

Then Nicky's face took on this peculiar beatific glow. Transformed he was. Followed his eyes to the mic. There stood a lanky girl with auburn hair and a face that had seen the places in life you're not supposed to look at with eyes wide open. And what eyes they were, green and flecked with gray. You know it's funny, she was way more than the sum of her parts where as what's-her-name was so much less. I suppose that's not fair, but fuck fair, where is the fairness clause in anything? Haven't fucking seen it. You?

Nicky, who just minutes ago had shouted a toast to the Yankees that drowned out the punchline of a joke the guy at the mic had been working on for an eternity, was now shushing the crowd.

"Yo, keep it down! The lady's trying to sing here."

And sing she did. Did two powerhouse numbers: Neil Young and Tom Waits. Her singing was a reflection of herself, a lot more there than met the eye. Brought the place down. The whole time I'm watching Nicky. He won't look at me. Before I can say something, he's off. Whatever had turned him zombie earlier in the evening, whatever the Jim Beam couldn't touch, was now forgotten. He'd taken the red-headed cure, hard.

Nick might've taken the cure, but it hadn't taken to him. She'd sent him packing. He was soon reacquainting himself with his old pals, Jim and Sam. Was positively wounded. A little boy again. Even what's-her-name gave him a smile. That was a rarity. Told Nick to lighten up on the drink, that he was apt to do some damage if he wasn't careful. Said he wanted to do damage. Great. Offered him a cab ride. Offered to dump my date so we could hit a club. That's when the offers stopped.

He was smitten. I knew the look. Being a zombie was easier on the heart, softer on the soul. Even if he wasn't already half in the bag, Nick wouldn't have wanted my advice on the subject. But on the way out, I checked with the bouncer, asked after the singer. Gave me her vitals. What's-her-name actually showed a bit of jealousy at that, a bit of fire. Unfortunately, the fire didn't extend past the bedroom threshold. Where would my life be without distant women?

Billy Wilder, the famous Hollywood director and producer, was told by a friend that a colleague had suffered a severe heart attack. To this, Wilder said, "Impossible!" The friend wanted to know why Wilder thought this so. "Because to have a heart attack, one requires a heart."

ANOTHER DAY, ANOTHER job. Well, maybe a bit different. Sunday was a rare time for what Boyle had put on the schedule for Nick and myself. Was working hard on my future lung cancer. Had graduated to Pall Mall. Smoking those nails was like working the heavy bag in the gym. It was filterless Camels next. My ultimate was these French bastards I'd seen. Gitanes or some such shit.

Was resting my ass on a Buick Electra 225, the same model as that fat fuck Finney used to drive. Had Nick steal it for me, not for irony's sake, but for convenience. Couldn't have it traced back to me. No rust on mine, pristine. *Nice work, Nicky.* Why that model? I had my reasons. Had my reasons for putting plastic slipcovers on the seats as well. Nick showed an hour late, of course. Had that half dead look on his puss that said he'd just seen his dad. Family meals at their house were like a steel cage match.

"You're late."

Smirked. "Scored last night, did you?" he asked after what's-her-name.

"We fucked, but I wouldn't call it scoring. My hand's more present when I jerk off."

"That good, huh?"

Flicked my cigarette high so that it spun, perfect as a twirler's baton.

"Had to check for a pulse," I said, opening the passenger side door. To him, "You sure as hell didn't score."

As I pulled out into traffic, he said, "Shannon, that's her name."

Course I knew that. Knew a fuck of a lot more. One advantage of my new fangled cop-ness was that I could have people checked out, day or night, the whole year through. It's amazing what you can get if you just label things correctly. If I'd asked to have this woman checked out because my friend was interested in her, they'd have told me to stick it up my ass. Called her a "person of interest" and got the full report. Almost surprised it didn't include the type of tampons she used. Didn't let on to Nick. Couldn't. Acted impressed. Was. When I'd left Rocky's, Nick was raging.

"You're shitting me."

Proud. "Nope, I got her phone number too."

Let it sit for a minute while he fiddled with the radio. Wondering where to take it.

"I know her." Mistake.

"Yeah?"

"She used to run with an old buddy of mine." Yeah, right. Like what buddy besides Nicky would that be? "She's got a kid, retarded I think. Something like that. And I hear she's a real ball buster, too." I think I also might've called her a broad. Like that's something I ever do.

Was losing it. It was like I was trying to protect somebody here. Her probably. Wanted to show Nick pictures of Kathleen and scream, "Leave this woman be, Nick. Look what the fuck happens when women get involved with people like us. And for chrissakes, bro, they didn't even fucking bury her!" Maybe I wanted to protect Nick a little bit too. Pulled the big Buick up in front of a deli.

Smiled. "Broads," was all he said. "No one calls babes broads anymore."

Not sure anyone called them babes either.

"What's the job?" he was curious.

"Shithead in the deli owes some vig," I said, grabbing my lower back. Hadn't been right since Finney shoved me down the stairs. But what had?

Nick worried. "Gonna be a problem?"

Let go of my back and grabbed the door. "Let's find out."

Deli man was a beefy boy with attitude enough to slice into sandwiches. He gave us the tough guy routine. Wasn't in the mood. Threatened his kids. Didn't worry about it. Hey, you going to play the heavy, be heavy, don't fuck around. Deli man got a little offended at that. Jumped the counter and I stuck a knife in his neck. Just enough to scare the shit and money out of him. Nicky thought I'd slit his throat. Nah, a trick I picked up in Philly from one of my training officers. Still sounds funky, training officer.

Took an apple out of the fruit basket as I came back over the counter. Ate it in the car. Sour piece of crap. Tossed it out the window and lit up. Back to the heavy bag. Saw the disdain in my old pal's eyes. Tough shit, bro. Guess I wasn't on his favorites list today.

"Boyle doesn't much like you," he said as if it would break my heart.

"Who the fuck does?"

When Nick turned away, I put a hand on the left side of my chest.

Nothing.

"Let us learn in order to teach.
Let us learn in order to do."

—Hebrew Prayer

HAD PLANNED TO wait for retribution, but the shelf life was shorter than expected. Even with the echo and sway that passed for my life, I had the sense of time closing in. Could not point to anything and say why. Just heard my internal clock ticking. O'Connor and Cousin Ira had their plans, not that the rest of the universe was listening. So I changed the plates on the Buick again, and let everyone know I was off to Philly for a few days' fun.

Fuck Philly, like I might go there for fun. For a haunting, it was a fine place. Could throw on my green coveralls as a nod to old time's sake and stand across from the old walkup, trying to catch glimpses of Leeza's ghost. Christ, she'd lately been coming back into my sleep. Even through all the blood and chaos, she persisted. Her presence, which had been but a buzz since Boston, had re-emerged. Hated myself for letting her back in.

With Kathleen, it had been so free, so frequent. Whatever we wanted, we got: no mind games, no *mishegas*, no withholding, no negotiation. We'd drink and fuck and fuck and fuck. No wonder it took her murder to make me miss her. Leeza Velez meted herself out to me in tiny rations. Being with her had felt like anything but freedom. I mean, for fuck's sake, I'd only been inside her three times and damn me if each stroke, each kiss, each thrust didn't feel like a prayer to an attentive god. It was to laugh, no? I may have let her spirit back in, but she was gone.

Philly it was, if only to establish an alibi. Parked the Buick downtown, rented a Toyota and checked into a motel that specialized in privacy, prostitutes, and triple-X programming. Called a bouncer I'd befriended when Leeza and I were doing our bar thing. Gave him a grand, key to the car, use of the room. When he came in, I went out. Did a reverse Beatles, leaving through the bathroom window. Caught a cab back downtown, got in the Buick, headed for Boston.

Crossing the Charles River didn't feel a fucking thing like home. Didn't love that dirty water, the beer or the baseball team. Just hated the Sox a little less than the Yanks. For a Mets' fan it's like choosing between gangrene and leprosy. They both get you, one just quicker than the next. Thinking on it, I wasn't so sure why I'd taken on the Red Sox mantle. Funny phrase that, as Mickey Mantle was the most beloved Yankee of all. First thought it was as much to rub it in Nick's face as to honor Kathleen. Nah, that was too easy. In my guts I think it was a warning. Like *Pay attention, Nicky, I've changed teams. I've gone over to the other side.*

Rudi was a slippery fuck and more clever than me by half. That argued against careful planning and surveillance. If I'd tried to follow his movements for more than a day or two, he'd sense it. You don't get to be such a kingpin cocksucker without the feel for being watched. An amateur like me couldn't set his ass up. He'd have one of his boys put one behind my ear and I'd never see it coming. Had to be done like a surprise party with only one guest and the guest of honor. Chances were good I would get myself killed in the process, but fuck if I wasn't going to take Rudi with me for company.

Drove to the warehouse where we first met. Parked down the street, way down, watched the cars leave until there was just Rudi's old Caddy keeping the cobblestones company. Hadn't seen any cameras during my first trip and I didn't figure Rudi was a surveillance camera type of guy. No, figured him as strictly old school, the type who liked that his rep would keep people away. Also didn't strike me as a man who liked tapes and records. Bet you he never wrote shit down. Kept it all in his head.

Took one last look around, knelt down, stuck a blade into the front tire of Rudi's Caddy. Strode right into the warehouse as I had that first time, quieter though. The crudely painted step van was still in the loading bay, maybe dustier, probably hadn't moved an inch. Looked up. Saw the light on in the office.

Shouted out, "Rudi!"

Saw his face at the window, smiling. Waved me up.

We were alone in the office. Wasn't smiling now. Smelled trouble. So I confirmed his fears to relax him.

"I'm fucked, Rudi. Didn't know who to come to. And I figure you owe me a little something for. . ."

Relax he did, as long as the woes appeared to be mine. "What's the trouble, boyo?"

"Cops. Think my best bud in New York has gone over."

"Jaysus. Nothing worse. Did ya go to Boyle?"

"Can't. I'm the one got my bud into the crew."

"Fooked three ways to Sunday, ya are. But what is it ya think I can do for ya?"

"Just need a few days to figure things out. Have you got a safehouse or something, someplace I can go and get my head around it? You owe me that."

He didn't look pleased. Rudi wasn't a man who liked owing people. On the other hand, you need more than fear to inspire loyalty. My sense was that he kept his word even when it killed him to do so. That was a big part of a man's rep, his word.

"Two days," he said. "No more."

Smiled as if he'd commuted my sentence. "Thanks, Rudi."

"Let's be on our way."

Shut the lights and locked the door behind him. Followed him to his Caddy.

"Shite!"

"What?"

"Flat tire."

Acted twitchy, nervous. "I can't stay out in the open like this. I've got my car down the block."

Sneered at me. Could tell he thought I was a fool. Cars are easy to trace. I was more trouble than I was worth. He only knew the half of it. Walked down to the Electra.

Actually stopped and admired it. Didn't make the connection between it and Finney's rusted piece of shit. Got in behind the wheel. He slid in next to me. Didn't wait or give him a lecture. Reached over and stuck a twelve inch chef's knife through his liver and pulled it across him widthwise. Yanked it out. Dark thick liquid poured out of him as he sat there frozen and in shock. Pulled away from the curb.

"You should have buried her, Rudi. You should have fucking buried her!"

Took out my shield and mashed it into his face.

In the movies, he would have smiled knowingly or laughed sardonically. In real life he coughed up blood and died. Plastic slipcovers are like a godsend. Found a spot to finish the job I started. Did what needed doing, then headed to Philly. Was back in New York a few days later when the story broke in the Boston rags

HUMAN REMAINS FOUND IN ZOO

Like I said, he should have fucking buried her.

"He didn't come here for answers. There were no answers. There was only sensation. No answers, and there would be no closure."

—George Pelecanos, *Right as Rain*

CHANGE IS SOMETHING I never dwelt on. Now it dwells on me.

Remembered my high school physics teacher explaining the myth of solidity. Told us to imagine the distance between the nucleus of an atom and its closest electron as the distance between the sun and Pluto. Not very comforting that. Said that solidity was a rationalization to help us get out of bed every day. Who wanted to live in a world where your next step might sink into the space between Pluto and the sun? Good question. Well, whether I wanted it or not, it was my new world.

When I got back from Philly, the lay of the land had once again changed. Was as if Boyle had waved his magic wand and Nicky was transformed. *Presto chango, abra cadabra.* Gold Rolex on his wrist, new suits on his skin, new apartment in Tribeca, new distance from me. Oh yeah, there was that freshly broken nose of his. Asked him where he got it.

"Saks Fifth Avenue."

Cute.

Or was it Boyle at all? Maybe the new woman, Shannon? Had she waved the magic stick? Doubted it. Didn't strike me as the type for silk suits and style, especially store-bought style. More likely she was the one to have broken his nose.

Frankly didn't give a rat's ass about the style changes, but Nicky's refrigerator friendship was disturbing. Thought we had reached some kind of understanding in spite of our recent troubles, Nick and me. Knew that what I'd done to the deli man had bugged him and my not drinking with Boyle

. . . Thought I was losing it, getting out of control. Maybe I was. Wonder what he would have thought if he knew I'd just assassinated Rudi and supplemented the diets of several zoo animals with pieces of the bastard's remains. Wondered if Vinny Podesta would try to knock me down now.

Had my answers soon enough. Met Nicky at Moe's Tavern in the old neighborhood. Guess our streak at Axel's had run its course. Moe's was run by Micky Prada, a good man, bullshit not a word in his vocabulary. Ran Micky's forever, never seemed to change. We aged. He didn't.

Nick was at the bar in his Armani suit. Looked good on him, complimented the fading bruises around his nose. Just didn't seem very comfortable, fidgeting a bit. Said my hellos, grabbed a beer and sat myself down next to the clotheshorse. Took one look at his eyes and understood the discomfort. Coke. Not one of my favorite drugs. Spend the whole evening trying to get as high as you were in the first fifteen minutes. Never works. Only get further away from that original rush.

"Doing lines in the men's room, huh? Getting a taste for the finer things, that it?"

He made some lame excuse about decent booze.

"Booze my ass. The pupils of your eyes, they're pinpoints. Only one thing does that."

Leaned in close to me, sneer on his puss.

"That one of the things they teach you at the Academy, one of those cop instincts you've developed?"

Christ. Cover'd been blown. Instead of panic, a kind of peace set in. Fucking relief it was. Didn't have time to worry how it'd happened.

"So you know about that."

That set off a chain reaction in Nick that was as good as any laser light show on the planet. Full range of emotions washed over his face in such rapid succession that I lost track. First there was an almost stunned admiration. Point is, rage was at the end and it stayed put.

Signalled to Micky. "Another round."

Nick nearly exploded. "I'm not freaking drinking with you, you . . . traitor, damned turncoat."

Smiled, but the cool, calculating smile. Cassius had nothing on me. Seemed Nicky and me had been working up to this moment our whole fucking lives. Didn't move my lips. The smile said it all. Grabbed his arm. Didn't like that.

"Listen up, hothead," I whispered. "You listening?"

Said yes.

"You think you know Boyle, but you don't. I've met some of his partners. The cops have been on his tail for a long time. That guy I popped in his apartment, he was one of ours. Had to make you believe. If you believed, Boyle would buy it. This is big. The prick and his partners are in bed with the border gangs in Mexico, using some of the profits for IRA operations." Took a drink. Took a breath. "So Boyle made me. What's he want, you to waste me?"

"Fuck you!" Nicky spit. "He reamed me a new one, yeah?"

"Whoa, buddy," I said. "I got your back."

Sucked down his drink and of all things said, "All the goddamned lies, the Red Sox, that part of it too?"

Almost smiled, then Kathleen stabbed me in the heart. Said something lame like they were going to take the series in a few years. Not much conviction in my voice.

"Do me a favor?" he asked, exhaustion his latest mask.

"Name it."

"Get the fuck outta my sight. Now!"

The rage was back. Good.

Said to him, "I'm here for you, buddy, but if you're thinking of running with Boyle and offing me, think again." Threw down some cash and headed out the door.

Was out, not gone. Waited in my car for Nicky to come out. Wasn't sure what he might do. Doubted he'd go to Boyle, but there was a long range of other possibilities. Truth was, he was as fucked as myself. More so.

Saw Nicky come out, the rage subsiding. Chill getting to him, buttoned up. Heard the pop. Looked away to see what it was. Tires screeched. Turned back to see Nick slumping against Moe's door, blood gushing out of his chest.

* * *

MUST'VE BEEN QUITE a sight, me sitting there with a shotgun by the side of Nicky's bed.

"Come to finish the job?" he croaked.

"Asshole. You think *I* shot you?"

"Did you?"

Poured him a glass of water. Probably shouldn't have, but didn't see a *Nothing By Mouth* sign anywhere.

"Wasn't for me, shithead, you wouldn't be here giving me grief."

Tried pouring some water down his throat and nearly drowned him. Hey, you try pouring anything with a shotgun in your other hand and let's see how you do.

Nicky's mother like barreled through the door.

"My baby, are you all right?"

Christ, the bullet hadn't killed him but the embarrassment nearly did. Turned like fifteen shades of red. Didn't have time to enjoy it. She turned on me.

"And where were you, you shit, where were you when they were pumping my baby full of holes?"

Nick tried to get her attention. "Mom, I'm, okay, really."

That really set her off. Sat and listened. Nick too. No choice. We both seemed comforted by the shotgun. Last resort, of course.

" 'We were pretty good friends once,' he said unhappily. 'Were we? I forget. That was two other fellows, seems to me.' "

—Raymond Chandler, *The Long Goodbye*

THAT TIME IN the hospital with Nicky's mother pouring it on was like being back home. Don't know about Nick, but I was only half-listening. I remember that in spite of my folks, my childhood had been a good one. Spent most of it outdoors, beyond the walls of the Rosen Asylum for Empty Lives. Remembered the summer days when the moms, not Sophie, of course, would group together on someone's stoop. We happily lived in the gutter and the schoolyard. We could weave a world out of asphalt and chalk. Now we lived in our own traps. Held incongruous shotguns in our hands.

Some detective named Ortiz came by to ask Nick a few questions. Waste of time. He would stay silent even if it was Boyle *vis-à-vis* Griffin that sent him a lead love letter. Nick would want to see to it himself. Me too. Rules of the street.

O'Connor met me at our usual spot. Wasn't thrilled with my having been turned out. Acted pissy. Like I wanted to get exposed, right? *Yeah boss, I even had a bull's eye painted on the back of all of my clothes to make Griffin's job easier.* Might've been relieved to have it out there, but I wasn't glad to become a fucking target. O'Connor gave me marching orders. I was to lay low and see how things with Nick would shake out, then it was out of town again till the time came to testify.

In spite of their high hopes for me, they hadn't been able to build the grand case they had envisioned. Boyle's crew would go down, that was certain. Maybe a few peripheral guys at JFK and the Port of Newark as well. But the big conspiracy case, the one reaching from Brooklyn to Boston, Belfast to the Mexican border, that was shot.

"Don't fret, lad, your job is secure," O'Connor assured me, a look on his face as if he'd been digesting glass shards.

As if it mattered. Thanked him anyway.

"What are the flowers for?" he wondered.

"I've thrown up on her grave twice. Sonya deserves a little something else from me this last visit."

Shook his head. "Dead is dead, lad. She's beyond caring."

"I'm not."

That hung there for a few seconds, him pondering the fact that inside he was nearly as dead as Sonya Einstein.

"Nicky's gonna need a place to run."

O'Connor started humming a tune that was familiar to me, but that I couldn't put a title to.

"What's that you're humming?"

" 'My Old Kentucky Home.' We're way ahead of you, lad. Why do you think I asked you to hang around? I'll have a package with the details delivered to you later today."

Watched him walk away. When he was fully out of sight, I placed the bouquet on the grave. Didn't do an apology. Picked up two rocks. Placed one atop Sonya's headstone, one on my mom's. It was Jewish tradition that. Explain it? Can't. It would be like trying to explain how the fuck I got here in the first place.

* * *

THE CALL CAME. Nick was fucked. Join the club.

Not even a hello. "I'm in deep shit."

Said, "You've always been in deep shit, Nicky, but needing help, that's new."

We met in a diner in Manhattan. Aren't any real diners in Manhattan, just money vacuums dressed up to look like them for the tourist trade. Like everything else in the city, you want reality, you go into the boroughs. That's where you find New York. Only authentic thing in Manhattan is the bullshit.

"Eggs over easy, I think." Only in Manhattan could you call two eggs for $9.95 easy.

Nick was busy pouring Jim Beam in his coffee. Christ, if he didn't look scared. Wasn't the bullet hole in him either. No, something else was at him. Suspected I knew what that something was.

"Shannon's husband was shot to death last night. My guess is it wasn't you. Tell me I'm right. You did that, even I can't help you."

Just sat there, drank his high octane coffee. The burden of speech was still on my shoulders.

"Griffin? A set up. Let me guess. You do me or they fuck you?"

Nick looked impressed. Not an easy thing to pull off.

"Never really wanted this life, but I've got a talent for this cop shit."

Impressed ran to desperation. "What am I going to do, Todd?"

My opening, slid a packet across the counter to him.

"There's a small town in Kentucky. I have a buddy there." For a guy from Brooklyn with one friend in the world, I seemed to have old buddies spread out over the country like dandelion spores. "He'll give you a job. Lie real low and we'll see to things on this end. There's some cash in there and a ticket for a train outta Penn Station. Leaves tomorrow morning."

"What about Shannon?"

"I'll talk to her. You just get the fuck out. Things are going down. Now you're only a nuisance. We'll bring you back up for the indictments."

Horrified. "You want me to testify?"

"You have a choice? It'll be messy, bro, but I'll sort it out."

"And my parents?"

"Go see them tonight, tell them you're going for a fresh start. They'll be glad you're straightening out."

Nick, his old self returning. "That's it? I just split and what . . . wait?"

"You got it. You're out of it."

"I'll be moving on then. Any words of wisdom to speed me on my way?"

"Sure. You shoulda had the eggs. They're great."

And there was Nicky walking out of my life. Least, that's what he thought.

* * *

WAITED FOR THE splash, for the car to pull away. Typical fucking Nicky, effective but sloppy. The rage again. Griffin's pants had snagged on one of the pilings. The waterline was high and it wasn't much of a strain getting my hands on him. Pulling his dead, waterlogged carcass the fuck out of the river was another issue. Thought both my shoulders would tear apart. *There goes my pitching career!*

Got his body onto the pier, the skin no colder now than when he was drawing breath, his heart probably warmer. I weighted the bastard down good and trussed his ass up like a chained mummy. He'd come up eventually. They almost always do, but he'd be hell to identify. Liked thinking about him as fish food.

"Give my regards to Rudi."

Pushed him back in the Hudson for the long dive goodnight.

"I felt as though I'd lost something, lost it forever and I didn't even know what it was, had no name for it. Those are the worst losses we ever sustain."

—James Sallis, *The Long-Legged Fly*

2000

Milwaukee

Downer Avenue

December, late.

Milwaukee? Yeah, don't ask. Okay, ask. I don't give a fuck. Because it wasn't Philly, Boston or Brooklyn. A lot of places aren't like those places, but not unlike them in the same way as Milwaukee. Just something about the Midwest, tough to put a finger on. Everyone pictures it in winter, as it is now: sunless, snowy, gray, frozen. There's another Midwest that the rest of the country never dreams of in their philosophies. Like that? Paid attention in English, especially during Shakespeare and Frost.

Waited to make sure Nicky made it to Kentucky all right, had a long talk with Shannon and her boy. Cute kid, made me play catch with him. Assured Shannon that Nicky hadn't done her ex. Neglected to mention that Nicky had done the man that *had* done her ex. Didn't tell her she'd be under surveillance until Boyle was in Attica. Easy to see what Nicky saw in her. Who knows what the fuck she saw in him? Who knows what a woman sees in any man?

That done, got in my car and drove west. This is fucked, I know, but I was following the Mets. Wanted to see a game in Wrigley Field my whole life. It's an ancient park, reminiscent in its quirkiness if not in style to Fenway. Scalped a sweet seat. Rained out. Figures. Thought Chicago was a pretty place, but it was too much like New York. Cleaner maybe, smaller with bad pizza. Still, had a subway and too many tall buildings for me to stay. Next stop for the Mets? Milwaukee. Me too.

Like Shea, County Stadium was an old piece of shit. But unlike Shea, the stadium food was great and there was a cool, new, retractable roofed stadium being built in the parking lot to take its place. It was supposed to be open already, but while they were building it a crane or something collapsed and like killed a few guys. My bad luck continued. Not so bad, I guess, as those poor bastards got crushed by the crane. Seen their last opening day. Didn't have to scalp tickets at County. Some guy gave me a spare. Liked that. Liked that a lot. Liked it that the Mets won.

Decided to stay in Milwaukee for a week. Months later, still here. Found a place on Downer Avenue. Don't you love that fucking name, Downer? Sums it up. Lived just up the block from a movie theater and a bookstore and not too far away from the university. Gotten back into my reading. Go to the movies all the time. Summer was great, not crazy humid like back home. Lake Michigan is cool. Kind of like the Atlantic with Kalamazoo on the opposite shore instead of Galway. There's these weird silver fish, smelt or some such shit, that wash up on the lakeshore by the thousands. Like a Passover fucking plague. Passes for normal here.

Fall was short, like two weeks. Then the sun disappeared, replaced by snow and grayness. You think it gets cold back East? Fuck that! This is cold, brothers and sisters. Few more months of this and Brooklyn in February would feel like South Beach. You understand drinking in a place like this. Jack Daniel's and me became even better friends . . . best friends. Hadn't been about friendship before. Always a nod to Kathleen. Milwaukee changed that. Nights were darker here somehow, darker even than Boston. Leeza and Kathleen were ever present, Rudi too, the cocksucker. Just didn't have the energy to leave. Figured I'd live through the winter. Lived through worse, much worse.

Then one day, about a week ago, God lifted the fucking veil. Grayness burned away by the sun like a match through dark acetate. Still cold as an icehouse, but to feel the sun on my face was redemption, if only temporary. Bypassed the place down the block and walked over to this little crime bookstore near the lake. Christ, I'd been in bigger bathrooms. Thing was, the owner, this tall gangly guy with a Led Zep tee shirt, had a New York accent. Didn't mention it. Afraid it would break the spell. Handed me my bag. Smiled at him large. Probably thought I was queer. So what? The sun was out.

Two doors down, an Irish pub run by Germans. Sums up Milwaukee, that. Was about to order a Jack.

"What can I get for you?" barman asked.

"Anything but Jack Daniel's."

Didn't flinch. Put a can of Point beer on the bar with a glass. Never had something so mediocre tasted so fucking good. Whispered "Goodbye" to Kathleen. Threw a twenty down on the bar. Left. Barman didn't chase after me. Understood about not wanting to break a spell. Stayed outside until the sun became irrelevant. There's no delaying darkness. Least, that's what I thought.

Put my key in the lock, night falling over my shoulder.

"We're in love, remember?"

Fuck! I *was* losing it. The weather was getting to me. My redemption was at end. The hauntings were back. Fumbled with the lock. If Nicky could only see me now.

"I'm gonna freeze my tits off if you don't open that lock!"

Leeza.

Forced myself to turn in spite of the spell.

Eyes had aged, if nothing else. Brightness dimmed. What had they seen? Mouth still dangerous, magical. Coat, hood, and gloves hid the rest of her. I stood frozen, not from the cold. Single tear leaked out of her left eye. Wiped it away. More intense than any kiss.

*　*　*

TWELVE YEARS OLD again. Her too, this time. No pretense in her smile. She was acting, she was pretty fucking good. Didn't care. We circled my apartment like two tentative boxers feeling each other out.

How'd you find me?

Guessed.

No, really.

Have my ways.

Get you something to drink?

Yes . . . No. What do you have?

What do you want?

Lawrence Block, huh? When did you start reading this stuff?

Boston.

How'd that go?

You didn't hear?

Hear what?

Told her about Kathleen, about the men I killed. Told her about Rudi. Realized I'd just confessed premeditated murder to a U.S. Marshal. Bright, huh? At least I hadn't done it in writing.

Leeza was silent for a moment, weighing it out.

"Good. Hope the lions didn't get indigestion."

"Oh, I spread Rudi around. Tigers, snow leopards and cheetahs got some too."

Her smile made me weak. Vanished. Her turn.

"Remember that Friday night, the call I got before we went out?"

Like asking me if I remembered my own name. Shit, remembered everything about that night. Just said, "Yeah."

"It was Rick's C.O.—"

"Rick?"

"My husband."

"Husband. You're—"

"Not anymore. Not since that night. His C.O. was calling to let me know he was killed."

"Killed doing what?"

"I don't wanna talk about it."

"But—"

"Okay, it's like this, there was a weird kind of symmetry in my life when I was living with you."

"What?"

"Jesus, Todd, you can read but can't you read between the lines?"

"Guess not. I'm sorry anyway."

"The marriage was already a victim of our choices. We were all over the place, hardly ever saw each other. Love doesn't sustain you. That's bullshit. You have to sustain love. When you stop sharing lives the love crumbles. Pining lasted a little while, but it just turned to anger. Everything does." Sounded like Nicky. "You start resenting even the things you used to find charming. Then there was you."

"Is this a reading between the lines thing again?"

"I'll have that drink now," she said.

"Jack, okay?" Nodded.

Brought it to her. Looked at my other hand.

Puzzled, "You're drinking beer?"

"Jack and me, we parted ways today." Explained about Kathleen, Jack and the Red Sox.

"Love her, Kathleen, I mean?"

"Wasn't about that."

"It is for me."

Didn't speak again until the next morning.

That night in bed, held on tighter than I've held onto anything or anyone, our mouths close enough to breathe in each other's thoughts. Eyes open, the both of us, for fear of slipping away. Rocking inside her, I prayed hard to that attentive God.

Woke up. Still night. The world smelling of Leeza Velez. Understood somehow about symmetry.

EPILOGUE

"The shadow of the blackbird
Crossed it, to and fro.
The mood
Traced in the shadow
An indecipherable cause."
—Wallace Stevens, *Thirteen Ways of Looking at a Blackbird*

LEEZA

FROM THE BENCH on the Promenade I looked up at the severe blue skies and out across the river where the towers used to stand and where yet another part of my heart is buried. I'm not sure how many more pieces I can spare. Sometimes I think back to my intro philosophy class at CCNY and the futile exercise of trying to prove a negative. I couldn't do it then. Can now. This is me pointing across the river.

I have always loved cloudless, blue skies. Like rainy days too, but for me there is proof of God in blue. When I was young and all the other kids speculated about beams of sunlight cutting through the clouds as heaven-bound souls, I knew better. Souls flew on blue days so they could clearly see the welcoming face of God. Nothing has happened to me that has shaken that belief. Yet, even as I sit here, the sun warm on my brown skin, I have to confess that blue skies now come with a caveat. Things other than innocent souls fly on perfect blue days.

There are days I fall into the trap of thinking things could have been different. Sometimes the differences are on a grand scale, like if there had only been fog that morning. Other times it's on a very personal level like when I wake up wishing Todd had tripped and broken his goddamned leg getting out of the shower that day. All are saved or some are saved, but in the end the calculus is wrong. Nothing was different. Nothing is different. Nothing is going to be different. That's me pointing across the river, again.

Boyle's time was at hand. Nick and Todd's as well. From the second they chose the life, they chose their deaths. I used to talk to the men I guarded about this stuff. A lot of them were not so different than Todd and Nick, guys who, for whatever reason got swept up in the world of violence and easy money. Some were stone killers, Griffin prototypes. They were easier to understand. The guys like Todd and Nick, they never had much to say. It was as if they were at some destination, but vague on how they got there or why they had gone in the first place. The hardcases had no such puzzlements.

Anyway, Boyle had been lost without Griffin. He'd gotten sloppy. In that life, a fish-eyed killer made a better right hand than a battered copy of the Good Book. Boyle had become a blind man wielding a chainsaw who saw neither the forest nor the trees. Lacking Griffin's sense for which trees needed culling, Boyle laid waste to landscape. Enemies were everywhere. Along with rats like Todd's Uncle Harry, Boyle's loyal soldiers were felled. And the case which had been faltering when Nick and Todd had gone their separate ways, was now a big fat federal RICO case.

The shame in all of it was that Boyle's worthless stinking life was to be spared. In exchange for his testimony and full cooperation, the prick was getting the full Sammy the Bull treatment: a few years in federal prison done in isolation and the rest of his time in Witness Protection. Sometimes you won't find justice anywhere in this world but in the dictionary.

Both Todd and Nick had been called back to give their depositions and to give testimony against the men Boyle had ratted out. For the most part however, they were there to give credibility to Boyle's testimony. It had come the full circle. In the end, they were still working for Boyle. Ironic? There was enough irony in the situation to gag on. After Boyle did his federal bid, it would be my employers, the U.S. Marshals that would be protecting his sorry ass. Even now, they had him stowed away in some cheap hump-and-run motel out in Sheepshead Bay.

Nick had been a lot more pleased with his recall than Todd. While Nicky had gone almost mad with the joys of small town Kentucky, Todd and I had settled into a happy life in Milwaukee. I was still on leave from the service and Todd. . . Well, he was still in limbo. He was a detective, but in name only. No matter what he'd done to bring Boyle and Rudi down, he was still the kid, the cowboy from Kennedy Airport in his heart. Oh yeah, there was this one other detail—I was pregnant, very pregnant.

Todd had pleaded with me to stay at his dad's house. "Makes my dad happy, watching over you and the kid," he said, rubbing my belly. "You are the only things that have made him smile in years."

"I'm coming with you," I said.

"But—"

"I want to meet Shannon. I'm coming."

He'd lived with me long enough to recognize I couldn't be swayed once my heart was set on something. Even I couldn't do much about it. When we were living together in Philly, I tried to not fall in love with him. I knew it was the wrong thing to do, but it didn't seem to matter. Then I tried staying away.

The plan was to meet Nick and Shannon for coffee on Chambers Street and then walk down to the Trade Center together. But as Todd kept reminding anyone within earshot, Nick operated on a different schedule than the rest of the known universe.

"There's Eastern Standard Time, Greenwich Mean Time, and Nick Time. Fuck!" he said, exasperated. "Let's go."

As we got near Vescey Street, somebody started yelling, "Hey, Detective Rosen, slow the fuck down."

Nick was darting through the crowd, a pissed off looking red head trailing a few feet behind. Todd tried to keep going, but I yanked his arm and we stopped.

"Yo, bro, I've missed you." Nick embraced Todd and whatever anger there was melted away.

"Ah fuck, me too. Christ, it's good to see you, man."

I introduced myself to Shannon.

"Look at you!" Nicky said, rubbing my belly. I didn't mind. You get used to it after awhile.

Shannon was more reserved. She hadn't had the months with Nick that I'd had with Todd. The ground upon which she walked was less stable. And my guess was that as much as she loved her boy, she had to suffer mixed feelings in the presence of a pregnant woman, her heart a jumble of resentment and concern. I didn't much like how she was looking at Todd. She seemed angry at him somehow, as if she blamed him for taking Nick away from her. I don't know, maybe I was reading too much into it. She had to know that, in his way, Todd had saved Nick's life. For that, I suppose, she hugged him fiercely.

Todd checked his watch. "Shit, it's time we get up there. Come on."

I gasped in pain. I mean pain like I was shot. Shannon grabbed my arm and held me steady.

"What is it? Todd asked, latching onto my opposite arm.

I'm gonna have a fucking baby right here in the fucking street. "Nothing."

Shannon said, "Bullshit! It's a contraction."

"I'll be okay," I lied. "They're just Braxton-Hicks contractions, like a false start. I've has these on and off for weeks. You guys go on ahead. Get this stuff over with already. I don't want it hanging over our little boy's head."

"Little girl," Todd disagreed.

"Go!"

"Go!" Shannon seconded. "I'll take care of her."

"You sure?"

"She's in good hands, bro," Nick said, leaning over to kiss Shannon's forehead.

"Okay," Todd agreed, but not eagerly.

I watched until they were swallowed up by the thickening crowds.

"They're gone, right?" I asked.

"Yeah."

"Good, get a fucking cab."

"Shit!"

Shannon had seen my skirt soaking through and the puddle at my feet.

Ten minutes later, as the cab jerked along West Street, Shannon said something about me looking fully dilated. I was way too busy screaming "Fuck, it hurts!" to remember exactly what she said. The shadow of a giant bird darkened the cab's windows.

"What's that noise?" I remember asking that.

* * *

THE SUN WARMS my face only so much these days and I grow weary of pointing across the river. I never get tired of looking into the depths of the blue sky. One day, I too will float weightlessly to heaven and see God's eager face.

"Come on Nicky, let's get back to the house."

There had never been any argument. If the baby was a boy, we were going to name him Nick. And Todd was clear that if it was a boy and if we named him Nick, that he would always know why and never have to question who he was.

Ken Bruen is the two-time Shamus Award-winning, two-time Edgar Award-nominated author of *The Guards*, *Once Were Cops*, and *London Boulevard*. He divides his time between Ireland and America. Visit him online at www.kenbruen.com.

Reed Farrel Coleman is the two-time Shamus Award-winning, two-time Edgar Award-nominated author of *The James Deans* and *Soul Patch*. He lives on Long Island. Visit him online at www.reedfarrelcoleman.com.

A Fifth of Bruen:
Early Fiction of Ken Bruen

By two-time Edgar Award nominee Ken Bruen.
Introduction by Edgar Award nominee Allan Guthrie.
Trade paperback, $18, ISBN: 978-0-9767157-2-6

"[A] beautiful book... [T]his is a must have for all [Bruen's] fans."
—Jon Jordan, *Crimespree Magazine*

"If you love complex, thought-provoking work, then you'll find something in this collection to intrigue you. If you love Bruen, there's no doubt, you'll already have cracked the spine."—Russel McLean, *Crime Scene Scotland*

"[*Funeral*] is the novel Samuel Beckett might have written, if he'd been a Galway Arms regular... *A Fifth Of Bruen* is a must for all true Bruen fans."
—Kernan Andrews, *The Galway Advertiser*

Contains Ken Bruen's early novellas & anthologies:
Funeral: Tales of Irish Morbidities / Martyrs / Shades of Grace / Sherry and Other Stories / All the Old Songs and Nothing to Lose / The Time of Serena-May / Upon the Third Cross

Busted Flush Press books are available from your favorite independent, chain, or online booksellers.

Please visit
www.bustedflushpress.com
bustedflushpress.blogspot.com
Twitter: bustedflushpres
for BFP news, author tours, book excerpts, contests, giveaways, and to find out what's coming from BFP next.